OLD TAPPAN PUBLIC LIBRARY, NJ

3 9144 09067631 4

OCT - - 2007

D0166849

Closed for Repairs

by
Nancy Alonso

Translated by Anne Fountain

Curbstone Press

A Lannan Translation Selection
with Special Thanks to Patrick Lannan and
the Lannan Foundation Board of Directors

First Edition: 2007
Copyright © 2007 by Nancy Alonso
Translation copyright © 2007 by Anne Fountain
ALL RIGHTS RESERVED
Originally published in Spanish as *Cerrado por reparación* by
Ediciones Unión (Havana, Cuba), 2003

printed on acid-free paper by BookMobile
cover design: Susan Shapiro
cover image: Fabrik Studios / Index Stock Imagery

This book was published with the support of
the Connecticut Commission on Culture and
Tourism, the Lannan Foundation, and
donations from many individuals. We are very
grateful for this support.

Library of Congress Cataloging-in-Publication Data

Alonso, Nancy, 1949-
  [Cerrado por reparación. English]
  Closed for repairs / by Nancy Alonso ; translated by Anne Fountain.
-- 1st ed.
    p. cm.
  ISBN-13: 978-1-931896-32-0 (pbk. : alk. paper)
  ISBN-10: 1-931896-32-1 (pbk. : alk. paper)
  I. Fountain, Anne, 1946- II. Title.

PQ7390.A435C4713 2007
863'.64--dc22   2006030702

published by
CURBSTONE PRESS 321 Jackson St. Willimantic, CT 06226
      phone: 860-423-5110   e-mail: info@curbstone.org
                  www.curbstone.org

"Big problems require big solutions."
Popular saying

"The solution to a problem changes the nature of the problem."
Peter's law (From Murphy's Laws)

"The world has always laughed at its own tragedies, that being the only way in which it has been able to bear them."
Oscar Wilde

Contents

PREFACE

Closed for Repairs is a series of eleven vignettes about contemporary Cuban life. The work is fiction but all the stories reveal problems of everyday life and especially the tribulations faced during the special period. The last story is called "Closed for Repairs," just like the book's title, and sums up the previous problems in a clever fashion. The head of an agency who is preparing for an official inspection of his department realizes that, on the all-important day, virtually all of his employees are going to be absent. Their excuses chronicle the situations depicted in earlier stories: transportation problems (lack of buses), lack of water, a medical test, an accident caused by a pothole, preparations for a trip abroad, arrangements for a baptism, efforts to keep a roof from leaking, and the unexpected illness of a pig being fattened. To top it off the phone won't make outside calls so he can't cancel the visit. Faced with a crisis, he is saved when an older man—a grandfather of triplets—brings him a CLOSED FOR REPAIRS sign. The sign had been in front of a day care center that had just re-opened and the grandfather offers the sign as a gesture of appreciation for the bureaucrat's help in solving the day care problem. The sign, in turn, becomes a solution for the dilemma posed in the last story. The agency head loosens a support beam in the reception area so that it leans, tells the typist to go home, and closes the office. As he heads out he puts up the sign saying CLOSED FOR REPAIRS.

Alonso's short stories not only show a cycle of frustrations—the book begins and ends with the same words—but reveal that the problems call for ingenuity on the part of the individuals facing the situations.

The book shows a spirit of resolve on the part of Cubans and is imbued with a sense of humor. Alonso's work, full as it is of distinctively Cuban expressions and situations, is also a description of everyday struggles that anyone can appreciate.

Anne Fountain

To my parents, always the first readers

CLOSED FOR REPAIRS

THE EXCURSION

The deadline was one o'clock in the afternoon. That's why M. had gotten up at 5:00—so there'd be enough time. Felicia was not going to pardon a lack of punctuality again. Too many times before she'd been left waiting, and M.'s excuses seemed more like unbelievable tales of horror and mystery than bitter reality.

A piece of paper written with care the night before was lying on the nightstand near the bed, and had the list of things to be done before leaving the house. It was important not to forget anything. Reading over the list, M. noticed that it didn't have the word rope. How in the world could the rope have been overlooked?

Until a little after six, M. was in the kitchen, first fixing a hearty breakfast—gulped down in haste—and then preparing what would be taken on the excursion. M. wrapped up the two pieces of bread with tomato, put the lemonade in the large thermos and poured what was left of the coffee in the small one. M. closed both lids tightly and placed everything carefully in the backpack. Then it was time to take the bucket of ice cubes from the freezer, put the cubes in a nylon bag, place that bag in another bag and then another one and wrap it up like a package—so that it looked like a real ice pack, the kind M.'s mother used to fix to alleviate headaches. M. put it back in the freezer so that it would be ready to go. Consulting the list again, M. began to check off what had been done. The bottle of water would stay in the refrigerator until just before it was time to begin the excursion.

Then M. turned to getting dressed and taking stock of accessories: comfortable shoes, Bermuda shorts, T-shirt, cap, and dark glasses. The list said two handkerchiefs but M. decided on three. Into the backpack went deodorant, number 30 sunscreen, the little containers of aspirin and diazepam,* the ulcer medicine, the anti-smoking pills, two packs of cigarettes, a box of matches, a lighter, six Johnson & Johnson Band-Aids and a fan. Also added were: Kundera's book, *The Unbearable Lightness of Being*, two newspapers from the day before, a deck of cards, the walkman, four cassettes and eight batteries, a magazine with an un-worked crossword puzzle, and the manuscript of a story M. hadn't finished. Finally, M. took a small folding seat and tied it to the side of the backpack.

M. looked at the piece of paper again wanting to make sure that everything on the list had been included. All that was left was to take the things out of the refrigerator, tuck away ten pesos in fifty and twenty-five centavo coins and pick up the map of Havana.

Leaving at seven o'clock on the dot with the heavy backpack in place, M. thoroughly studied the map. On it M. had drawn red circles marking the places within a two-kilometer circumference where public telephones were located. Now the excursion would be underway to find one that worked. M. held out hope of speaking to Felicia before one o'clock.

The Excursion

The rope. M. had forgotten the rope and went back to get it. This time if the call didn't get through on time M. would resort to a self-inflicted hanging. It would be the ultimate solution for the never-ending saga.

*An anti-stress medication (generic Valium)

3

CAESAR

It was during that time when all of us in Cuba raised or cultivated something. The fall of the Berlin Wall and a proliferation of cages, corrals, and fences on this island took place at the same time. While Europeans were tearing down barriers, here we were putting them up. It was a question of survival.

Living on the fifth floor of a building imposed an additional challenge to my family's initiatives. We planted—restricted by space—in improvised flowerpots. But the pots had good dark soil and were well cared for by my grandmother, who carried out a strict regimen of watering, administering nutrients, and dispensing affection and soothing conversation. She moved the pots in search of optimal light and did battle with whatever plant disease came along. People who came to visit were amazed at our greenery. And even though we sometimes felt claustrophobic surrounded by so many plants—there were nearly a hundred in the apartment counting the cactus and the bonsai guava tree that had been grandfather's pride—we never lacked for condiments in our meals, some kind of salad, and herbs for everyday aliments. What turned out to be difficult was finding *what* to cook and, above all, how to satiate our carnivorous needs. There was almost nothing! Nitza Villapol, the ineffable Nitza—Cuba's famous culinary queen—helped us with her books and the TV program *Meals in a minute.* She came up with some truly memorable recipes; some of her own making and others invented by people's ingenuity. There were grapefruit rinds seasoned and breaded as if they were steak; little rolls of cabbage and bread crumbs served in sauce as if they were meatballs; pasta elbows boiled, set out to dry and then fried in a little oil, as if they were deep fried pork crackling; squash puree strained as if it were tomato; and a thousand and one ways to make croquettes out of potato or yuca as if they were of ham. But a substitute no matter how good is always a substitute and the original is the original.

One day father came home from work, shouting:

"Come here everybody!"

He would round us up with his macho authoritarian style, something we women in the household "maternalistically" allowed whenever he wanted to talk about something important. Gathered around him we listened to the familiar refrain.

"I can't take it anymore! I'm fed up, really fed up with all the *as if it were* dishes. I need real food," he said continuing his diatribe. We looked at him compassionately but without saying a word. Poor *papá* was not just thin; he looked like a cadaver. He was the one who had it really bad because every day he had to bike, round trip, the fifteen kilometers between home and his office. Mother on the other hand, worked at a child care center right in front of my high school and just a few blocks from the house. And grandmother's only obligations were on the domestic front.

"This simply has to end," said *papá*, adding what turned out to be a novel twist in his catharsis. "I've decided that we're going to raise animals." He paused to take in the effect of his declaration. But mother and grandmother did not give up any ground and just stayed quiet, letting him, like always, gallop off with his crazy dreams. All the while they were searching for the weak link in his theories so that they could then trap him with question after question until poor *papá* gave up the scheme and never discussed it further. Never have a mother-in-law and a daughter-in-law been so perfectly aligned. "For several days now," father resumed, "I've been consulting with experts. Now I'm ready to discuss which of the options is best."

The rabbit project was the first one to fail, in spite of an ingenious plan for hanging cages divided into various levels (to save space), water dishes that refilled automatically, and a whole set of reproductive calculations that father had made.

"And who will be responsible for getting the grass?" asked grandmother.

"I'll take care of the cleanup, the mating, the parasite control," said father.

"I'm asking about the grass, my angel, the grass," specified grandmother.

"That would be something difficult for me to get, mamá. I leave early in the morning when it's still dark and I don't get back until night. I thought that maybe you could cut some around here," he said.

"Have you forgotten about my arthrosis and damaged sciatic?"

"I suggested it precisely because I thought it would help you get some exercise," argued father.

"Is that all you think of all my chores in this household? I try to do my part and not to be a burden, my angel, but now to ask me to go trotting around looking for grassy patches with a sack slung on my shoulder…" Here grandmother's voice sounded cracked and she seemed on the verge of tears.

"All right, it's OK mom, don't get like that." Father hastened to console her wearing a guilty look on his face and searching out in mother and me a support he did not find. "Let's forget about the rabbits."

The next idea was getting baby chicks that were being allotted in the ration book. We would put them in little coops warmed by light bulbs instead of maternal warmth, fatten them with feed given to us by father's cousin, kill them when they reached an optimal weight and leave enough offspring to produce eggs and to continue the line. It seemed like a good plan. Father promised to take care of the animals and swore that we wouldn't have to put up with any bad smells. All he was asking for, poor thing, was our approval and then we'd all enjoy some good slices of chicken.

"And what do we do with Cleopatra?" asked mother in a worried tone.

Cleopatra was our Siamese cat. He'd been given to us when he was young and we didn't discover that he wasn't a female until after he'd been baptized with the name Cleopatra. Once the mistake was discovered, father did the unspeakable and tried to rename Cleopatra Julius Cesar. Unfortunately he never managed to convince the cat of the new moniker's advantages and had to resign himself to using Cleopy, a name with ambiguous sonority but which could at least be recognized. I think it was probably at that point that our family began to gain notoriety in the neighborhood. It was quite something to see the neighbors' faces when they discovered that Cleopatra was not a female.

"What do you mean, what should we do with Cleopy?" asked father with note of surprise in his voice.

"Have you forgotten that Cleopatra is a great fan of feathers?" continued mother using a questioning technique taken straight from the Socratic school of inquiry.

"Well he'll have to learn to live in peace with the chickens," countered father.

"You really think so?" I ventured as all four of us turned toward Cleopatra who was comfortably ensconced on father's armchair—the best one in the house.

Father took a few moments looking at Cleopatra, before sighing deeply and answering me:

"No."

The proposal to get a pig was accepted without objection, probably because of a premonition. Father had talked it over with Antonio, a neighbor on the first floor who was also interested in raising animals. They agreed to fence in a small plot at the back of Antonio's apartment to set up a pigpen—just like other tenants who had staked out claims over similar parcels without so much as an "if you please" from God or the authorities. To start with, there would be two pigs, one for each one, and they would share the tasks of keeping things clean and finding food.

"The only thing I'm asking the family to do is collect some portions of unappetizing leftovers, which you can probably get at the day care center or the school," said father. "We'll put up with the ripe smell and disgusting appearance as the price to pay for meat on the table and honest to goodness pork cracklings, *chicharrones*.

The day that father brought him home, Caesar was a

recently weaned piglet and just a *piglet*—not yet Caesar. The name came later. Our first impression was that he was like a puppet with jerky and awkward movements. The fact that he was an albino added a nice touch, and perhaps his cute little snout and the pink hooves helped account for the future turn of events.

A week after having arrived and exactly on the day that he was going to be "fixed," Caesar suffered the first diarrheas. None of the home remedies worked and poor *papá* had to carry Caesar in the basket of his bicycle all the way to the Veterinary School. The doctor on duty explained that it was just a digestive irritation and that Antonio's pig was OK because it was of a sturdier breed than our Caesar. He prescribed a plan calling for injections and a healthy diet and recommended taking the utmost care in matters of hygiene.

"It's best to bring him up to the apartment until he gets better and where I can look after him" offered grandmother. Nobody opposed the idea; in fact we all applauded her willingness to save the weakened piglet.

And that's the real reason we didn't get Caesar castrated and why he came to live in our home. All the other versions are just idle talk and gossip.

Grandmother gave Caesar his injections and fed him with a baby bottle until he was considered out of danger. She would give us an update on his progress (he was still called the *piglet*) in our after dinner chats. There were clear indications of improvement when Caesar began to accept Cleopatra's invitations to play; I never in my life imagined that a pig and a cat could hit it off so well. And we all knew Caesar was feeling better when he began to perk up anytime he saw grandmother beginning to fix supper.

"Well mother, if he's fully recuperated, it's time to take him back down and let you get some rest," suggested father. He had just heard from grandmother how the little animal was eating everything and had gained at least ten pounds. "And what if he gets sick again?" asked grandmother. "That's silly! He's just a pig not a calf," said father. "Tomorrow I'll take him to Antonio's patio before I leave for work."

And so he did, without suspecting that that very night he would find Caesar in the middle of the living room. Grandmother explained to father what mother and I already knew: she had gone down at noon to give him something to eat and, when she found the *poor piglet* making squeals of fright, she knew he must be feeling bad and brought him back.

"Besides, my angel, no matter how much you work at cleaning, that pen is always dirty and foul smelling. I could never eat a piece of meat that came from such a place," said grandmother, backing up her argument with a look of utter disgust.

"But all pig pens are like that," said father.

"What you don't see can't hurt you," replied grandmother. "But I've already seen…And I'd like to have a little more time to work with him up here," she concluded.

Giving *piglet* the name Caesar was my idea. The name was short and sonorous and gave poor *papá* (who'd lost out on the name Julius Caesar with the cat) the possibility of having an emperor in the house. Tying a red kerchief around Caesar's neck was mother's decision. She claimed it was to keep away envy and evil thoughts. Whatever mother's motivation, the kerchief was probably another reason for the wagging tongues in the neighborhood.

Nobody imputes intelligence to pigs the way they do for cats and dogs. Caesar learned to take care of his "needs" in a box in the patio, to respect the plants, and to recognize the proximity of every member of the family before we entered the apartment. Grandmother, who was the author of all information about Caesar's progress, remarked with frequency:

"When it comes to animals you need patience and perseverance. What could one expect of a pig treated like a beast, closed up in a pen, without any space, and left with nothing to do all day except eat?"

And as Caesar learned to obey everyday orders, such as "Caesar come here," "Lie down," and "Let me stroke your tummy," we stopped talking about fried chunks of pork and father continued to bring home dishes of the "as if it were" variety. Thus when Caesar got to be one hundred pounds we faced a real dilemma.

"We're going to have to decide what to do with Caesar," said father.

"You're not thinking of killing him, are you?" asked grandmother while mother and I accused father of murder and told him not to even dream that we would eat a slice of pork or a *chicharrón* that came from Caesar.

"Who said anything about killing him or making a meal of him?" said father offended by our insinuations. He had been the last to grow fond of Caesar but, at last, he, too, had been won over by the animal's affability. "It's just that he's very big and worse yet, he'll keep on growing. The time will come when we won't be able to keep him in the apartment. I've thought about giving him to a friend who has a farm; we'd have a guarantee that he'd be kept for reproducing. It's a good thing that we didn't castrate him."

"And could we visit him from time to time?" asked grandmother.

"I suppose so, although the farm is far away."

We tried to convince ourselves that the farm was a grand solution even for Caesar, who would be elevated to the status of stud animal. And apparently we succeeded in fooling ourselves. So father went ahead and made all the arrangements for the transfer.

The flaw in the plan was that they arranged to come and get Caesar on a Sunday at mid-morning when all of us were at home.

Father took Caesar downstairs with a rope around his neck instead of the red kerchief while we watched from the balcony. But the moment grandmother saw them loading Caesar into the pickup truck, she shouted:

"Don't take him away!" just like the supplications of the grief-stricken when the moment comes to remove the dead person from the funeral parlor. And she rushed down the stairs accompanied by Cleopatra and gave Caesar a hug.

Mother and I followed as far as the second floor and beseeched grandmother to calm down and come back. But before we knew it we were supporting her, to the amazement of our neighbors who had flocked to their windows and balconies. After all that, *Papá* just didn't have the heart to let Caesar go. He asked the friend to forgive him for the bother before climbing the steps again with Caesar and Cleopatra playing between his legs. Grandmother, mother and I followed them, climbing the stairs arm in arm and crying from shock and joy. I suspect that the entire spectacle did much to nourish the legend that was being spun about my family.

We eventually left the building not because of the

rumors, but because we were able to move to a ground floor apartment and have access to the space out back, which we enclosed, covered and cemented. Caesar gained the new space at our expense because in making the move we lost a room and now grandmother and I sleep in the same room. Although we've thought about a female companion for Caesar, we still don't know what we'd do with the offspring.

Father had gotten Caesar used to a nightly walk even when we lived in the other apartment, because he didn't want the pig to get sedentary. Now, in our new locale, when Caesar's ready for a walk, he stops in front of the door, moves his head toward the harness and poor *papá* gives in. People who've never seen such a curious scene exclaim:

"Why look! There's a man walking a pig as if it were a dog!"

And my father always says. "Why this pig: it's as if he were a member of the family."

AN INFORMAL VISIT

The idea for the visit came up during a convention in Havana. The just-named minister who hailed from Morón asked for the town's representative and Ovidio stood up.

"Fill me in about my hometown," said the minister. But before Ovidio even began to answer, the minister continued: "Is it true that our Rooster *sings better each day*, just like the famous tango singer Carlos Gardel?"

At that, everyone laughed. Everyone except Ovidio.

"The recording is new, comrade minister. At six every morning and six every night, right on the dot, you can hear his song in all the surrounding areas.

"Did all of you know," said the minister, turning to those present, "that Morón, our Morón, and the Morón de la Frontera in Spain are the only cities in the world that have raised a monument to the rooster?"

For more than half an hour Ovidio had to endure an onslaught of questions. It had taken many mornings without sleep to prepare for the convention, and had he known that the minister was a fellow *Moronense*, a man from the very same town, he would have spent even more time in preparation.

"Tell me, do they still celebrate the Day of the Absent Moronense?"

"Why, yes. In fact we've revived the tradition."

"Well, why don't you invite me this year?" interrupted the minister.

"But, of course, comrade minister, it would be an honor for us to count on your presence on that day." responded Ovidio.

"And, when is it?" asked the minister, writing down in his agenda the date that Ovidio gave him.

"The invitation will give me the chance to see childhood friends and revisit places I remember with fondness. Since my family and I moved to the capital when I was twelve years old, I've never been back. Now I have the chance to return but not *with a wearied brow* like the words of the famous tango." And this time Ovidio managed to join the chorus of chuckles.

"Get in touch with the head of my office and the two of you can coordinate the visit," said the minister to Ovidio. "But nothing formal, mind you."

"Of course, comrade minister."

When he got back to Morón, Ovidio informed the local authorities that the minister had accepted their invitation to visit the city on the Day of the Absent Moronense. He was congratulated on the initiative and chosen to preside over the organizing commission of the upcoming celebration.

Ovidio worked up what he himself described as a program of renewal and restoration. He selected his collaborators—thirty-three in all—with care and grouped them into five sub-commissions: Gastronomy, Culture, Sports, Decoration Ceremony, and the Minister's Detail.

In the first meeting he expounded on his ideas and explained the timeline that would control the sequence of preparations. Reports would be rendered in plenary sessions held every fifteen days, and, in addition, every week Ovidio would meet with Luis, who would be responsible for carrying out the details of the minister's visit.

"We have just six months to carry out our project and there'll be no last minute improvisations, especially in regard to the details concerning the minister himself. I've already found out which places he would like to visit. And, Luis, let me tell you the man is a fanatic about our Rooster, so you need to make sure that on the big day the Rooster's as finely tuned as Gardel." At that point everyone broke into a big laugh. Everyone except Luis.

The heads of each planning group lined up their strategies and created their work brigades (Supplies, Transport, Community liaison, and Maintenance among others). Besides their own initiatives they were obliged to satisfy all needs pertaining to the minister. Ovidio had made that very clear from the start.

"Luis is coordinating the visit and the rest of you have to back him up."

The owners of the home where the minister was born collaborated with enthusiasm to embellish the house. All the façades of that block were repaired and the access streets were paved with asphalt.

"But," said Ovidio to Luis: "I think it would be a bit much to put up a plaque to note the minister's birthplace."

Fortunately, the primary school where the minister had studied was in good condition and had new desks.

"In any event, we'll take a look at the building before his visit. It's lucky the minister didn't do his high school work here because that building is really run down."

The Tango event was scheduled to take place in the town's main cultural site, the *Casa de la Cultura*, and the musicians were given typical gaucho clothing. Thanks to the spirit of encouragement and enterprise and the cooperation of the aficionados of Argentine music, the place was decorated with photos of the most notable tango singers and an abundance of Cuban and Argentine flags. Somebody brought what was probably the only *mate* gourd in town, and someone else came up with the idea of using *tilo*—a Cuban herb--if they weren't able to find *yerba mate*.

"The minister doesn't even suspect that we'll have a "tangofest." That will be our pièce de résistance."

The conscripts, charged with cleaning up the area around the Leche Lagoon and spiffing up the soccer field, received a special pass in recognition of the magnificent work they performed.

"And this year we'll have the best Aquatic Festival in the town's history. Not even the time when the minister's father was a boy can compare with what we're doing."

The refurbishing of the Rooster turned out to be phenomenal. Two restoration specialists brought expressly from Havana gave new luster to the bronze figure. Other experts carefully reviewed the synchronism of the audio component, and fifteen days prior to the visit the Rooster was shining like new.

"Now we just have to make sure that he can really perform on schedule."

The restored train station recovered the prestige it had enjoyed when it was the pride of the town. No more burned out light bulbs and timetables that hadn't been updated. The thorough cleaning and installation of abundant wastebaskets made it possible to appreciate the beauty of the floors. The availability of running water eliminated the cobwebs that had accumulated on the plumbing fixtures of the public bathrooms.

"Having the train come from Ciego de Ávila to Morón is an excellent idea," Ovidio told Luis. "But it would probably be best if all the visitors, and not just the minister, arrived by that same route. Therefore the banners at the train station should say: "A fond welcome to all absent *Moroneros*."

On the day of the celebration, the guests arrived, just as had been planned, at ten o'clock in the morning. At the platform of the train station a welcoming committee, along with the municipal band, and flowers proffered by the most outstanding young pioneers greeted the visitors. Ovidio gave a brief address. Carriages, pulled by horses adorned with garlands of plastic flowers, were waiting on either side of the park to transport the retinue to the locations that were hosting festivities.

"I can't tell you how much I appreciate this visit, Ovidio," commented the minister after the return to his old neighborhood, the soccer match, the outing on the water, and the picnic lunch on the shores of the lagoon. "I'm not sure what you have planned for the rest of the afternoon, but I'd really like to visit the old high school."

"The high school!?" Well, it's not ... I mean, you never studied there" replied Ovidio.

"That's true, but my father was a professor of history in the days when it was an Institute with upper division classes and I used to love to accompany him. I remember those classrooms and hallways, so spacious and clean."

"The problem, comrade minister, is that there are classes in session and we'd be interrupting, and now it's just a high school for basic classes and the students are very young," pleaded Ovidio.

"That doesn't matter. I'd like to go by for just a moment."

"Well, we could go by for just a moment," repeated Ovidio. "But now let's head to the cultural event and then we can go by the school."

Taking Luis aside, Ovidio whispered:

"We've got to prevent this visit. I don't know how, but we've got to keep the minister from seeing the high school. It hasn't had a lick of upkeep in many years."

"I think I've got a solution," said Luis. The only thing I need for you to do is keep him away until five thirty." He added confidently: "Don't worry. I'll take care of the rest."

Spanish and African dances, heel tapping sequences, poetic improvisations based on rhyme, and a series of debates were all presented to delight the delegation of now-present *Moronenses*.

"And next we have a surprise," announced Ovidio, looking at the minister. "Our Friends of the Tango Event!"

The tango musicians played their gala repertoire and then spent a good deal of time playing songs that the minister requested. Ovidio also put in several requests until at last Luis arrived.

"OK, time to go! They're waiting for us at the high school," shouted Luis over the sound of the large concertina and to the consternation of Ovidio.

He smiled and flashed Ovidio a "Not to worry" look.

"Everyone to the carriages. Even though the school is nearby, we're going to go directly from there to the decoration ceremony at the entrance to town, at the foot of the Rooster."

In front of the high school a huge crowd of students was waiting. The minister, visibly moved, could scarcely make his way through the throngs of young people, visitors, and accompanying townspeople.

"I remember it as being more spacious," said the minister, while Luis whispered in Ovidio's ear: "I placed the tallest boys against the walls and used the welcome banners to good advantage. What do you think? You don't even notice the holes and the dirtiness." Then, without further delay, Luis gave the call to depart. "We've got to go now. Remember that at six o'clock the commendations are being awarded."

As they headed to the carriages, the minister asked Ovidio to include some of the boys from the enthusiastic school group in the retinue.

"We'll invite the outstanding students from each year," said Ovidio. "And the invitation will serve as a moral stimulus for their exemplary conduct."

At six o'clock sharp, after listening to the Rooster sing, the closing act of the day's festivities began. The minister turned to the students who had accompanied him and declared earnestly: "Thank you, thank you so very much for this warm welcome. I feel confident that you young people who are before me represent the new guard of the future."

To which one of them was heard to reply:

"For us it will be an honor to some day become absent *Moronenses*.

And at that, everyone laughed. Everyone except the minister.

THE TEST

Berta arrived at Central Havana Emergency Hospital before eight o' clock in the morning, although her appointment was for nine. She was so nervous that she hadn't been able to stay at home. She preferred to be waiting close to the place where they would do the test, the same one that last year had resulted in the diagnosis of her illness. She felt anxious not only about all the things they would do to her body but also about the results of the examination.

Two months before, Berta had begun to smoke something she never did, not even when she was an adolescent and wanted to put on grownup airs. At first she felt nausea when she inhaled, but after a week she could go through a pack of cigarettes in twenty-four hours as if she'd been a chain-smoker her entire life. She needed to breathe in all the smoke she could. And coffee, a swig of coffee, before every cigarette.

While she waited her turn, she went out to the street to smoke a few more times. If the test turned out well, she wouldn't be doing that again for another ten months, as the date for the repeat examination began to draw near.

When she entered the laboratory, she was helped to swallow the slender tube that would examine the condition of the walls of her stomach. She listened as the doctors evaluated what they observed, and most important of all, the conclusion: her gastric ulcer had not healed.

Berta tried to hide her euphoria. Her efforts with cigarettes and coffee had produced the desired effect. There was the ulcer, live and latent. This would give her the medical certification guaranteeing a dietary supplement to her ration book of basic food items. Now she could have another year of breakfasts with milk. Problem solved.

She tucked the valuable paper with the positive lab result inside her purse and spied the cigarette pack that she had kept hidden from the doctors. She would give it to someone with a nicotine habit because, she—that's for sure—wasn't somebody who liked to smoke.

IN THE LORD'S VINEYARD

With agile steps Troadio climbed the hill of the street that led to the church. He stopped at the top, as always, to gaze at the sight. He was moved by the simple construction, modest yet capable of sheltering the community of believers. But this time his beatific contemplation gave way to a startled expression when he saw an endless line of people in front of the sacristy at the side of the church. Never in the more than ten years that he had assisted Father Cosme had such a multitude gathered at the site.

It would have to be today, thought Troadio, the day that Father Cosme is sick and that I will be handling the baptisms for the first time; but if the Lord has given me this test, there's nothing to do but resign myself to accepting it. As he approached the parish church, Troadio implored: *Almighty God, through the power of the death and resurrection of Your Son, I beseech you to help this humble servant whose only desire is to serve you in increasing Christ's flock.*

As he entered the Sacristy, Troadio made his way through mumbled comments like "Who does he think he is?" and "Look at that old scrawny guy trying to get ahead in line,"— all referring to him. And, once inside, he reached a kingdom of utter confusion and disharmony. The sexton charged with the task of noting information needed for the baptisms was insistently asking a young woman for the name of the father of the child in her arms but getting nothing but silence as an answer. Several children were playing spades under the impassive gaze of family members who were talking very loudly, and two young men, faithful helpers of Father Cosme, were attempting to establish order but only managing to augment the clamor. Troadio had the sinking feeling that Satan must be lurking nearby.

"What's going on here? This is the house of the Lord, a place of peace!" exclaimed Troadio feeling full of the righteous indignation that had prompted Jesus to drive the merchants out of the temple.

"Everybody out! There can only be one person at a time with the child to be baptized. Everyone else must wait outside until they're called.

The sexton commented that perhaps the avalanche was because of the date, the seventeenth of December, the day of Saint Lazarus. Now I'm the one paying the price because people associate Saint Lazarus with Babalú Ayé, thought Troadio. Once again he called upon his capacity for acceptance and humility. He put on his alb, tied it with the cingulum, and placed the stole with a cross over his left shoulder. The spotless white tunic helped imbue Troadio with a sense of serenity. The habit makes the monk, he thought, reprising a familiar refrain, as he entered the church through a small door facing the side of the main altar.

The sanctuary was overflowing with people, and the deafening uproar took Troadio by surprise. For a few seconds he repeated to himself as a litany, *Almighty God, forsake me not*. Then, recovering control he asked for the attention of those present but found himself completely ignored. Finally

24

he managed to get the crowd to listen by letting out a strident "Silence nowwwww!"

"Without your help this baptism <u>is</u> impossible," said Troadio, lowering his voice. In truth he would like to have said that the way things were going, the baptism <u>was</u> impossible. "There are many children, and not everyone has finished getting registered," Troadio continued. "We must wait with discipline."

A stir arose among the congregants, and some of them rushed toward the sacristy. In the Lord's vineyard there are all kinds, thought Troadio. Some of them have just now understood that they need to be registered. He asked on their behalf: "Father, forgive them for they know not what they do."

"Now, may I please have your attention," said Troadio speaking to those gathered in the church. He noticed that most of the faces were completely unknown to him. "While we allow time for all the participants to get enrolled, let me explain a little about the ceremony. It's best if the parents, godparents, and the children here to receive the oil of consecration, the holy unguent, sit near the center aisle."

After clarifying that he had said *unguent* and not *urgent* and becalming the commotion among those who insisted that all were equally urgent, Troadio reestablished a semblance of order. Those who were mere spectators yielded their places to the protagonists. They did so in a manner that seemed rather unconventional by Troadio's lights, leaping from one bench to another and passing the children from hand to hand. But by the time you could say amen, the multitude, had, in its own way, gotten itself got reorganized.

"Please stay quiet in self-communion and meditation while I go to the back to help out so that we can begin more quickly," said Troadio, convinced that he had won the battle. Nonetheless, scarcely had he turned his heel to depart than he heard the stirrings of commotion again. He thought it best not to let on that he was aware and prayed silently: "Forgive them Lord, for they know not what they do." He'd take care of restoring order later.

When they finished with the godfather of child number fifty seven who said he was the last one, Troadio moved to close the sacristy door. Just then someone knocked insistently and Troadio replied: "Baptism's over!" And then he added: "That is to say, we're not accepting any more children; come back another day."

Troadio returned to the sanctuary escorted by the two young assistants and the sexton. Facing the rabble once more, he raised his arms and said: "Brethren, I need you cooperation. Today, as you can appreciate, we have a very large number of children. Besides that, Father Cosme is indisposed. I will be administering the sacrament for the first time in my life as a deacon."

He noted surprise and worry showing on some of the faces. Many have no idea of what a deacon is, thought Troadio, but if I stop to explain it, we'll never finish. So he decided to clarify by saying: "You may not know it but in case of necessity, any baptized person can baptize if his intention is to do just what the Church would do." He regretted uttering that sentence when he heard someone ask:

"So why are we here if we can do the same thing ourselves at home?"

"That would only be in cases of extreme necessity." emphasized Troadio. Normally it is the priests and the deacons who have this responsibility.

Troadio took advantage of the fact that they were listening to him with interest to begin the ceremony.

"First of all let us extend the embrace of the church to the neophytes and welcome their parents and godparents. Brothers and sisters in Christ, with rejoicing you have experienced in the bosom of your family the birth of a child. With rejoicing you come now to the Church to give thanks to God and to celebrate a new and definitive birth through Baptism. We join together today with joyful hearts because today we will increase the number of those baptized in Christ.

He was surprised at the effect of his words. There were shouts of happiness, applause, and even a shrill whistle that pierced his ears. Troadio understood that if he wanted to avoid major problems, he would need to shorten the ritual, do only what was essential and finish as soon as possible. Nonetheless, he couldn't keep from explaining that in a sanctuary jubilation should be expressed in a spiritual manner. He exhorted the multitude to show composure and respect.

"Now would be the time that you would tell me out loud the names of the children," announced Troadio," but it is best that we leave that for when they're baptized." He then went to the next step, reminding the parents and godparents of their responsibilities. "In asking for baptism for your children, you realize that you are obliged to bring them up in the faith." When Troadio got no reply he asked them to repeat: "Yes, we know," which was shouted out by all those present. "And you the godparents, do you agree to help the parents in this task?" A booming *yes* was the response, delivered along with nervous laughter and a ripple of commentary about how well they had handled the reply.

One of the parts of the baptismal ceremony that Troadio most liked was when the celebrant, the parents, and the godparents made the sign of the cross over the children. Among that confused crowd he realized that it would be impractical for him to get to each child, and therefore he decided that they would make the sign of the cross collectively.

"Children of the Lord, the community of Christians receives you with great joy. I, in His name, sign you with the sign of Christ the Savior." Troadio accompanied his words with an encompassing gesture.

"Now, you, parents and godparents, make the sign of the cross over the children." But when he saw that some were disconcerted and others where making the sign of the cross on the chest, he realized that he had to spell it out: "On the forehead; the sign of the cross goes on the forehead."

But the most disconcerted of all was Troadio, himself, when he heard one of the godmothers seated on the front row, tell the godfather: "Do it two times, once for you and once for me. Remember, I'm not what they call very religious."

The Lord's vineyard has all kinds, thought Troadio.

The liturgy of the word turned out to be difficult. Every minute that transpired seemed to increase the restlessness of the assembled, who were anxiously waiting for the blessed water to be sprinkled over the heads of those to be baptized. Troadio had selected as a Bible reading the passage from Mark 10, verses thirteen to sixteen, "Suffer the little children to come unto me." Now as he watched the playful forays of a group of children, Troadio thought to himself: The works and seductions of Satan are many and varied. He would have liked for those children to draw near to him so that he could give them the well-deserved smacks on the head that their parents had neglected to administer. "Free me O Lord from evil thoughts," he prayed.

Asking that crowd to keep silent was useless, Troadio observed. Anguished, he made a decision to accelerate the ceremony even more. He signaled to the two faithful young men who helped Father Cosme and who were to assist with the next step and told them: "I'm going to shorten the congregational prayer for the neophytes and the prayer of exorcism, and you won't be taking part."

Then speaking rapidly to the assembled public, Troadio announced: "When I tell you to do so, say, *Amen. Now brothers and sisters in Christ, we pray for these children who are to be baptized, for their parents, for their godparents, and for all those who are baptized.*" He paused briefly and continued: "*Almighty God, You know that these children will feel the temptations of a seductive world. Keep them from the power of darkness and guide them along the long road of life. In the name of Jesus Christ our Lord.* Now everyone say with me, *Amen*".

Before proceeding to the baptistry, Troadio was supposed to ascertain, through a liturgical dialogue that seemed too long given the circumstances, that the parents and godparents renounced Satan and were followers of Christ. *Forgive me God, but I know what I am doing,* said Troadio to himself. Then, in a categorical fashion and looking toward the godmother of questionable faith, he affirmed: "I take it for granted that all of you repudiate the devil and believe in the trinity. As a sign of acceptance, please say with me, *Amen.*"

Troadio felt his dominion over the audience and hastened to continue without transition. "Brethren, the moment you've been waiting for, the baptism itself, has arrived. First we'll call the children in order of registration, and their godparents will bring them up the center aisle, where they will wait in an orderly fashion until it's their turn.

The sexton handed Troadio the receptacle with the consecrated oil, one of the faithful assistants to Father Cosme read the list, and the other organized the line and area of approach to the deacon.

Once again the solemnity of the temple was disrupted. This time the blame lay with the names, many of which were so strange that it wasn't even possible to identify the gender of the one named. The young man who was reading took every care to pronounce clearly and complied successfully with his duty. For Troadio, nonetheless, disentangling those names, without having a written list before his eyes, turned into a kind of torment. In each case, he was supposed to ask: "What name have you given your child?" and he was obliged to repeat the sequence of sounds that he heard.

"Yosenqui, I baptize you in the name of the Father," Troadio made the first anointing with holy water, over the head of the child, "of the Son," his hand moved a second time, "and the Holy Spirit," the third time. Following Yosenqui were Ubisney, Yosleider, Odelvis, Siriannis, Diannettis, Ifreidi, Lidibet, Barneidis, Yurieski, Yuneisi, Yolexis. The few with names like Juan, Angela, and Mercedes gave the deacon a bit of a respite.

As Troadio anointed the succession of children, the level of the holy water went steadily down, until he feared that it might give out. The godparents of the last ones to be baptized protested that there was hardly any water left for them, and Troadio had to defend himself saying that a baptism was the same if it was done by complete immersion in a river or with a single drop of water on the head.

Another battle Troadio faced was with those who wanted a pictorial remembrance of the event and who, with both still and video cameras in hand, got in the way of the ritual. Grudgingly they agreed to pull back when Troadio promised that afterwards there would be a simulated baptism and they could take all the photos and videos they wanted.

Troadio observed with consternation that some families were beginning to leave and called to them to stay since the ceremony wasn't over. How could they be leaving? he thought. *Forgive them Lord for they know not what they do.*

"Now it is time to complete the baptism. *God Almighty, Father of our Lord Jesus Christ, who has freed you from sin and given you new life by water and the Holy Spirit, consecrates you with the chrism of salvation. As Christ was anointed Priest, Prophet, and King, so may you live always as members of his body.* Repeat with me please, *Amen.* Now if you'll stay in your places, I'll anoint each child with the sacred oil."

In the midst of total disorder, that neither the two young, faithful assistants to Father Cosme or the sexton could control, the deacon traversed the entire sanctuary and anointed the crown of the head of each child with the chrism. He suspected that some of those who presented themselves to him for anointing had not really been baptized. In particular he did not remember having seen the redhead, about four years old, dressed in a suit of very deep blue. Despite doubts and moved by urgency, Troadio daubed oil on all the heads that were placed in front of him.

Fortunately, there's not much left, he thought: the Presentation of a lighted candle, the Lord's Prayer and the Benediction. But the ceremony got bogged down when the deacon asked the parents and godparents to come forward with their candles to light them in the Pascal candle. Many had not brought candles; some because they did not know, others because they couldn't get them. One of the fathers, the one who had the video camera, was carrying a huge candle and he proposed that it be considered representative of all the baptized children. Troadio accepted the solution. It was a way to wrap things up.

"*Receive the light of Christ,*" he said, lifting up the Pascal candle. The father lit the collective candle, and as he placed it on the altar, accompanied by the sexton, Troadio continued; "*With you parents and godparents lies the responsibility to keep this light burning brightly. May your sons and daughters, enlightened by Christ, walk always as children of the light.*" Cognizant that some might interpret his words as the end of the baptism, he hastened to add: "Please don't go yet. We still have the Lord's prayer," in spite of which some, feeling very pleased with themselves, departed.

The prayer resonated with steadfastness until the final *Amen.* Troadio, exhausted, finished the baptismal liturgy with a *I bless you all, go in peace* that could hardly be heard and with a gesture to that effect that was understood perfectly by those present.

With what energy he had left, Troadio said he would do the promised simulation for those who wanted to take photos and videos of such a memorable occasion. And even though the baptism was over, he felt a sense of remorse for having baptized children whose parents were atheists, and probably children who weren't registered. No doubt children who had never been baptized received the Holy Oil, and not all those who were registered and baptized had been anointed with chrism. Some had left before the Lord's Prayer and the Benediction.

But, the deacon thought, with a sense of relief, he'd put the problem behind him. Forgive me, Father. *In the Lord's vineyard there are all kinds.*

MUTINY ON BOARD

To the people of Cojímar

There's probably no one in Havana more obsessed with buses than I am. Maybe as obsessed as me but not moreso. Fortunately, the decision I made after what happened today will free me from that burden.

My stubbornness about buses led me to memorize route schedules and even the telephone number of the main bus terminal to find out why they weren't coming by. I also learned the names of the drivers, as if the familiarity of a personalized greeting might prevent my hearing the dreadful declaration as I boarded the bus: "We're full. The last one aboard is this young lady." And the young lady would be the woman just in front of me, and I'd have to content myself with the scant consolation of being first in line for the next bus.

It's hard to gauge how much time is spent talking about transportation. When I set off for work in the morning, instead of the customary, "God be with you, daughter," my mother says "May you be lucky with buses today." My husband, unfamiliar with the torment of a daily commute because the refinery where he works has its own transportation, listens to my vicissitudes with con-

34

descension. And of course at the bus stop there are always commentaries.

"Are they running OK today?" ask the optimists.

"Have you seen one pass by going up the street?" specify the anxious ones.

"There's only one running today and it just went by," is the favorite line of the sadists.

"They say yesterday was Cachimba's day off—you know the driver of the bus that makes the last run—and there was no one to drive the bus. And then blah, blah, blah …," say the know-it-alls.

At the factory where I work, every single morning everyone has an anecdote about how he or she managed to get to work. We even have a kind of competition to see whose tale is most bizarre. In an odd twist, the longest wait is turned into a kind of victory with the compassion of the rest of us being the prize.

But don't think a passenger's troubles are over once he's on board. There might be a delay because the driver and the fare taker decide to have a snack break at a cafeteria or because of a breakdown in one of those places where it's practically impossible to get another bus. And there can even be surreal experiences, like what happens in Buñuel's film *The Exterminating Angel,* when no one can leave: the bus just sits there. Something like that happened this afternoon, and that was what set off the drastic decision I made.

It all began at the bus stop where route 58 begins its run. It was threatening to rain. Thick clouds darkened the sky and deepened the frowns on the faces of those waiting. A restlessness overtook the crowd. Nothing can break up a line like the prospect of a cloudburst such as the one threatening us. The ones in front are worried about losing an assured seat, while the ones at the back of the line see the possibility of getting one. A tall man with an organizing air took it upon himself to count how many of us there were and assured everyone: "Listen, there'll be enough seats for almost everybody so there's no need to break the line." The word *almost* was said without emphasis. "Don't forget that if there's a big hassle the driver won't let us get on."

The bus stop where we were waiting has a large laurel tree with branches for shade. They're useful as protection from a scorching sun but insufficient as a shelter from rain. When the first drops fell, announcing a deluge, we squeezed together around the trunk of the tree, carved with many names and hearts, and promised to maintain our places in line. We prayed to Saint Isidore, the farm servant, to take away the water and restore the sun. But minutes later rain was dripping down from the wet leaves and falling on us. While one group ran to take refuge in a nearby building, others went to a bus stop with a shelter in search of alternate routes. The rest of us stayed put, convinced that there would be enough seats for the drenched. The 58 is the only bus that goes as far as Cojímar, where I live, and thus I'm freed from the temptation of bouncing from one bus stop to another.

A young man with long hair sounded the alert when he saw the bus turning toward the avenue. We organized ourselves quickly and cheerfully in spite of the rain. We saw it stop about thirty meters away from us at the place where the route comes to an end. It seemed to take forever for the passengers to get off. Then to top it off we saw another group gathering at the back of the bus.

"They're employees," affirmed the organizer man, trying to calm us and calm himself. "Up to four of them have the right to board."

We counted, some out loud, as they got on. When we reached number five there was a degree of consternation. Nonetheless we stayed put, standing in line and dripping water. From that point on, every increase in the number of "employees," heightened our feelings of resentment and fueled our protests: "there can't be that many employees;" "how shameless they are;" and "here we are like fools getting wet." Our remarks bordered between surprise and anger until at number twelve someone ordered with a crisp shout: "That's enough. Let's get on board!"

We went running toward the bus and scrambled on board. Two old men and a man on crutches who was missing a leg were left straggling and were the last to get on. The seats gave out and five of us were left standing: the two old men, a woman loaded down with bundles, a man with a package under his arm and me. The man on crutches found that the seat reserved for the handicapped was still available and sat down.

"If it hadn't been for the cheaters who sneaked in, we'd all have seats," pronounced the lady with the bundles who was standing beside me.

"Well, we're all here. We just need to get moving," I heard the organizer man call out from where he was sitting.

"Everybody has to get off!" announced the driver with a menacing tone.

"What?" everybody answered at the same time.

"Just so you know, this is the only car on this line and we won't be getting underway until all of you get off and make an orderly line back there where you're supposed to be. That's how it's gonna be because of your lack of discipline," shouted the driver, without looking back. He sat with his eyes glued to the avenue where the rain was beating down.

"Say what? Have you gone crazy?" protested a bald man whose complaint was echoed by many of the rest of us.

"You're going to have to kill me before I get off of this bus and into that downpour."

"Don't be ridiculous. We've been waiting for more than half an hour and look how it's raining."

"My children are asthmatic, and they've already gotten pretty wet."

"The undisciplined one is you, the driver. You allowed a bunch of people get on while we were waiting over there in line."

The fare collector was the one who responded indignantly to the accusation.

"They're employees. Do you get it? Em-ploy-ees. And there were only four, just like the rules say.

"Don't be a liar, buddy. We all saw twelve people get on," said the bald man.

And that was when the free-for-all broke out. The fare collector went after the bald man, telling him that he was the real liar and shaking a fist in front of his face. The bald man, who was shorter, refused to be intimidated and repeated what he'd said. The fare collector invited him to step outside if he was a man. The driver intervened and advised the fare collector to back off:

"Be careful. Later on you could be the one in trouble for punching a rider in the face."

"Calm down, you two. It's raining outside and you could catch a cold," commented an older woman.

The alleged employees didn't say a word. They stared out the windows with feigned interest in something outside. Anyone could tell who they were because they were drier than the rest of us.

The driver and the fare taker began talking to each other and ignored our comments. Then they turned on a tape player real loud, either to unsettle us or to entertain themselves, I don't know which. The voice of Roberto Carlos drowned us out.

After a while the organizer guy stood up and said: "*Compañeros*, since it looks like the rain's letting up, why don't we just go to the bus stop, get in line again and get back on."

We could have eaten that guy alive, and with unanimity, except for him, agreed not to get off and to exercise passive resistance. It was matter of principle.

For a while we kept talking about how incredible it all was. Then the conversation gradually tapered off. A girl whose face was marked by acne began to do knitting. One of the old men started talking about soccer with the longhaired kid, who had given up his seat to the old lady. The woman with the bundles took out a casserole of chicken and rice and began to eat. I entered into conversation with the mother of the two asthmatic children, and so to each his own.

At this point the rain definitively stopped and the driver renewed his charge, over the sound of the voice of Roberto Carlos.

"OK. Now you don't have the excuse of the rain so please go to the bus stop and I'll pick you up there."

"And who's going to assure us that there won't be a retaliation and that you won't leave us stuck *there*?" asked the bald man.

"We wouldn't do that," replied the fare collector with a note of irony. Nonetheless nobody moved.

At the back of the bus two men appeared, and then a woman, and asked if they could get on. The fare collector said the bus wasn't leaving any time soon, but we told them just the opposite. We said the same thing to others who started arriving, and they all got on. Finally the driver decided to close the doors. The volume went up on the Roberto Carlos tape.

And, that's when the sweat bath began. The bus was one of those donations from some cold-weather country, and the windows were the size of thimbles. We were all sweating buckets but refused to yield to the new form of aggression, which only lasted a short while. Before long, the driver and fare collector couldn't take the heat and confinement any longer themselves and opened the doors. Some of the new passengers got tired and left. After that I lost count of how many got off and on. We veterans stubbornly stayed put.

"Please get up, can't you see I'm handicapped?" said a woman with dark glasses to the man with the missing leg, as she got on the bus.

"Me, too," was the laconic response of the man.

"Do you have an I.D. that identifies you as handicapped?" insisted the woman in the dark glasses.

"Can't you see that I'm missing a leg?" he replied with surprise.

"And, can't you see that I'm visually impaired?" She pointed to her glasses. "Those who belong to associations of the handicapped have priority, so if you please..."

Fortunately, a big mulatto took the blind lady by the arm and gave her his seat without saying a word, while she waved her handicapped ID as proof of eligibility.

One of the asthmatic children shrieked: "Mommy, look there's a peanut vendor!"

After the two children returned with their paper cones

filled with peanuts, the mother put one of them on her lap and gave an older man a place to sit.

The peanut seller was followed by other vendors. Several passengers got off to make their purchases. Others of us, fearful that the bus might take off, went to the doors and got help in arranging the transfer of money and purchases. I knew I'd be able to hold out better after having eaten a couple of filled pastries and a bag of popcorn. The moment of glory came when I was able to get some coffee from the hand of a plump woman who was standing nearby with a thermos of coffee and some paper cups. The driver and fare collector didn't buy anything. I saw them get off and enter a nearby building.

"And what if we take the bus?" suggested someone.

"Please, let's not talk nonsense," said the organizer.

"Are you afraid?" asked the bald guy with a mocking tone.

"Perhaps one of those employees could help us," I said with a sarcastic tone of voice, trying to rankle the ones who'd sneaked on.

Almost as if he'd guessed our thinking, the driver rushed back, running. He stopped at the head of the aisle in front of us and said that he was calling the main office to get instructions. We paid him no mind and continued eating, discussing whether the Cuban or Brazilian soap opera was better and commenting on how bad the endlessly-playing Roberto Carlos cassette was.

The fare collector arrived with a look of satisfaction on his face and informed us that their superiors had backed them up and that we would have to make a line again. People stopped eating. The discussions came to a halt. No more commentary about soap operas, music, soccer games and the

Cuban associations for people with handicaps. No more knitting of jackets of worsted yarn. The "you'll have to get off" routine was reprised, but of course no one got off.

As the songs of Roberto Carlos continued to play, the driver and fare collector whispered to each other. Then the latter disappeared into the same building where they'd gone before. We've won this small skirmish, and now we'll see what the next move is, I thought.

"Hey little brother, Oscar!" exclaimed the man with the package under his arm, hanging out of the back door. Oscar returned the greeting just as effusively, climbed on and both of them sat down to chat on the back steps of the bus.

When he came back, the driver told us that a car with an inspector sent by the main office would be coming to analyze the situation. And that's exactly what happened.

The inspector got on slowly and scrutinized us from behind sunglasses, which seemed pretty uncalled for since it was getting dark. Or could it be that he was visually impaired? With a sweeping gesture he ordered the tape player turned off, and at last we had a respite from Roberto Carlos. The elegant blue tie, pinned by a gold tie tack to a long-sleeved white shirt, with the collar protected by a checkered handkerchief, and the watch chain hanging from the front of pants whose back crease was impeccable, made it clear that the inspector was a man accustomed to order and neatness. He filled his lungs with air before speaking.

"*Compañeros*, let's see," was as much as he got out, because we didn't let him finish. We all talked at once. The asthmatic children took advantage of the confusion to throw paper airplanes made from the peanut cones; the woman with the bundles put her hands on her head; the lame man banged the floor with his crutches.

"Not like this, this won't work! One person speaks at a time," demanded the inspector.

The organizer tried to say something but he was interrupted by the bald man who explained what had happened, with the help of the young guy with the long hair. Seeing the impassive face of the inspector, I understood that our arguments would not convince him, and added my voice in a desperate attempt to see that justice was done. Nonetheless, nothing moved him and his conclusion was:

"This is a mutiny that we are not going to permit: either go back and make a line or we'll head for the Police Station on Zapata Street."

In the face of wavering from some of us, the girl with acne stood up so that we could hear her well and declared: "That's why we're here like we are, because we're sheep and we're getting what we deserve. We should all of us stay in our homes and refuse to go to work until they figure out how to fix our transportation problems."

The big mulatto guy answered her energetically.

"Sheep no, *compañera*. What we are is grateful. I am what I am thanks to the Revolution, and not even dogs bite the hand that feeds them." He turned towards the inspector and added: "Nobody's getting off here. We'll go wherever you want."

We all applauded the mulatto, except for the supposed employees and the man with the package who decided to get off. An old man commented to the young man with long hair: "It makes you wonder what he had in that package."

At last the bus got underway, although we ended up at the jail. The inspector got in his car and escorted us to the police station, where the driver and the fare collector, faces beaming, got out. Meanwhile we dug in waiting to see how things would play out and hatched a plan of action. The organizer was neutralized, and we decided to speak in this order: the bald man, the long-haired guy, I, and the mulatto, as representatives of diverse sectors of society. We debated if one of the asthmatic children, in the name of the Pioneers, should say something, but discarded the idea when we saw them asleep. Night had fallen some time ago.

About a half-hour later the driver, the fare collector, and the inspector returned, accompanied by a captain and a lieutenant.

"Good evening, *compañeros*," said the policemen greeting us cordially. "Please, we'd like to hear your version," added the lieutenant.

We rolled out our plan and it was just like we had practiced. When it was my turn, I couldn't believe how well I spoke. I was inspired and I even gave a brief history of the transportation problem in Cojímar. The mulatto said that after my participation, the only thing left to add was that they needed to do a better job of selecting workers able to interact with the public.

The captain asked which ones were the employees and we pointed them out.

"Please show me your employee identification cards," asked the lieutenant to the discomfort of the driver, the fare collector, and the inspector.

I have my card from the National Association of the Blind and Visually-impaired said the little blind lady, who appeared to be hard of hearing as well.

Of the twelve "employees," only three had a current I.D. card. Two showed cards from their time of military service, while the others said they didn't have the cards with them.

It was something to see their faces, above all when the

lieutenant and the captain spoke of fining the driver and fare taker, of sanctions for the inspector, and of the need to serve the working public. They said that the people without required identification would have to stand up before continuing the journey. We couldn't disguise our joy and shouted in support of the victory. The mulatto smiled when we sat down.

"People like you, with your sensitivity, are the ones suitable for this type of work," he told me.

As the bus began to move, we were surprised by a request from the little old lady.

"Why don't you put on some music?"

The driver made no attempt to humor her, and I believe that it was the long-haired guy who began to hum the Roberto Carlos song about a million friends. The other passengers joined in with an even better rendition of the chorus than the chirping birds of the original.

At the exit of the Havana tunnel the driver stopped the bus and said: "This is as far as we go. She's broken"
Like a spring, just sprung, the bald guy and the mulatto were out of their seats. And in the blink of an eye they were next to the driver.

"Crank it up right now or we'll do it ourselves," said the two men.

And their determination was so resolute, that the driver after doing a simulated adjustment continued the trip.

Every time one of us got off, there was a warm farewell from those of us who were still on the bus. We were like a special family, and we wished each other luck for the next adventures.

I got to my house about nine o'clock at night. Mother was at the doorway, very worried and with her blood pressure rising. My husband didn't understand how I could be in a good mood when I told him that the experience on bus 58 had been terrible.

"I'll tell you the story after I bathe. For now I'll just tell you that the experience today was the straw that broke the camel's back." And I added: "Oh, and I think I found a way to bypass the torture of the buses: I'm going to check into working for the Ministry of Transportation."

He looked at me as if I'd gone crazy. And I hadn't even told him that perhaps I'd be learning to drive, and I'd become the first woman driver of a bus in Havana. It would be the 58, of course.

THE STORY OF A POTHOLE

To Romelia
*To Rosa Ana de la Torrre**

It might have been just one more among the many burrowed in the streets of Havana. Nonetheless, it gained notoriety because of the geographic fatalism of having been born in front of the house where Noelia Torres lives. She discovered it one day, when it was still very small, when you almost fell if you stepped into it.

"No wonder the pavement gives way with so many water runoffs in the neighborhood. And just look how many times I've tried to get this dealt with."

Noelia went back to complain about the broken plumbing to Perdomo, the *Poder Popular* delegate—her neighborhood representative. He, for his part, gave vent to his own tales of woe: steps taken to solve that and other difficulties affecting the community— housing repairs, the poor condition of the children's park, the leaky roofs of the Polyclinic, and the dumping of garbage any old place—all without satisfactory results.

"I arrived ready to do battle but ended up offering consolation to the delegate. You can see that Perdomo really wants to work things out, but the bureaucracy won't let him. He needs our help."

Noelia wrote a detailed letter to the Havana Water Works office—with copies to the municipal government, the delegate, and the core group of retirees to which she belonged. She explained the situation and alerted the authorities to the fact that delays in getting things fixed made everything worse and increased the costs. The rest of the family helped her in the campaign. The son printed the letters at his work with paper that the daughter-in-law had somehow gotten hold of. The grandson was in charge of distribution, except for the copy of the letter going to the retirees group. Noelia delivered that letter in person during an extraordinary meeting that she herself had called and whose only item of business was to inform the *compañeros* about the battle that had begun.

Meanwhile, as prayers were lifted up and no miracle descended, the pothole continued growing at a healthy pace thanks to the every-other-day watering it received. In that zone, water arrived on alternate days. At the same time the fertilization of the pothole was accomplished with contributions of rubber from the tires of cars, trucks, motorcycles, bicycles, and strollers, and from the soles of shoes of people who stumbled into it.

Noelia wrote another letter, this time addressed to the municipal government, in which she complained about the incompetence and indifference of the employees of the Havana Water Works, to whom she sent a copy, along with one to the delegate and to the group of retirees. In this letter she described the deterioration of the asphalt as a result of the constant runoff. This was the first time that the word "pothole" appeared in one of her missives.

"And if this doesn't get the repairs done, we'll go higher

up to achieve our aim. Somebody's got to listen to us," Noelia declared.

At a certain point—no one knows just when—the pothole began to be known mainly through its nicknames: "the hole" and "the pit." Noelia, for her part, kept sending letters with their respective copies to those at many levels of authority. In each case she attached the previous reports so that the history of the pothole could be better understood. The pothole itself was growing its pedigree and adding to its resume, to the consternation of those concerned. Bones, tires and even broken shock absorbers were added. As a consequence, each new protest letter from Noelia required so much more paper that the daughter-in-law could no longer keep up with the demand. If Noelia's letter-writing war didn't end up in a pothole itself it was only because her neighbors went all out to provide reinforcements of paper.

Noelia was given appointments at various offices and was listened to by numerous officials. Everyone explained to her the difficult coordination required to undertake such works. The maintenance brigade for plumbing, the entity that would rightfully begin the work first, was not the same one that repaired potholes. In every office they lamented the scarcity of materials and promised that as soon as possible they'd find a solution to the problem.

Two years later, Noelia decided to denounce the situation in the state-run Havana newspaper, the *Tribune*.

"How good I looked in the photo, pointing to the pothole! Let's see if this article brings an end to our odyssey."

Noelia's heart attack was prompted by a notice informing her that that in order to contain the pothole's progression—and until a shipment of pipes from China arrived—they would proceed to close off the source of water that led to the problem. Therefore, those in her neighborhood would now receive "the precious liquid" from a tank truck, once a week. Noelia didn't get as far as reading that *her* pothole would be included on the map of chronic potholes published periodically by the Ministry of Transportation, in the magazine *Roadways.*

While Noelia was in the hospital, family members avoided talking about the pothole. She didn't mention it either, as if the earth had somehow swallowed it up.

Back home after being released from the hospital, it was inevitable that Noelia would hear about some of the misfortunes that had taken place that month. There was the resignation of Perdomo when the water brought by truck did not arrive because of a lack of fuel. The great victory that had been achieved, according to her grandson, was when water had gone back to being delivered through plumbing— just like before, one day on and one day off. Water continued to spill out onto the street because the pipes from China still hadn't arrived. Transit was interrupted because of the dimensions the pothole had reached. It was like a giant stomach, constantly devouring. Warning signs were put up to alert the public to the dangers. If anyone fell in, he might well end up in China—where he could check on the missing plumbing supplies.

"That tree that's growing in the middle of the pothole, is it a flamboyant?"

In the end, Noelia assumed responsibility for watering the pothole and the flamboyant on the days when the springs from Havana Water Works weren't flowing. Children in the neighborhood helped her to erect the fence and to put in other plants.

And now Noelia says: "I'll write to the Society for the

Protection of Animals and Plants, to the Council of State, to the ecologists of Greenpeace, and even to the United Nations if need be. But if no one pays attention, they'll have to go over my dead body to close down the garden I always dreamed of having."

*Friends of the author who have had pothole struggles of their own.

NEVER FINISHED

To Albertico Yañez,
who's always building

The drama was still hidden behind the innocent appearance of a stain, when Carmen discovered a discoloration on the ceiling of the kitchen. She didn't doubt that it was one more thing to be added to the long list of touch-ups needed in the house. The home was fairly well preserved, in spite of the long time since it had seen a paintbrush.

Times were different, thought Carmen. She remembered from her childhood that the smell of paint, the transfer of paint cans and the moving about of ladders, foretold the approach of the Christmas season and gifts on Three King's Day. From her parents Carmen had inherited the custom of embellishing the house for the traditional Christmas Eve supper and the arrival of the New Year. And even though money was tight sometimes, they insisted on exorcising the sorrows of the past twelve months with coats of whitewash. The New Year brought a new beginning and a fresh start was inconceivable with stains on the walls and ceilings.

That was before. Before paint and even paint thinner had disappeared from the market, before stains had become part of the house's décor, before Carmen's children playfully gave names to the various discolorations based on their shapes. It was similar to what she used to do as a child, stretched out in the garden, looking up at the sky and deciphering the capricious contours of the clouds. Except that in the cloud shapes a rider and horse might gallop off and be lost in the horizon—pushed by the wind. But the stains never came undone. They intensified and proliferated like this one that appeared on the ceiling of the kitchen just above the stove.

"In a house, you never finish," Carmen had heard her mother say from the time she could remember. But she hadn't understood the full meaning of the statement until it was up to her and her husband, Manolo, to assume the reins of the house. One day she found herself repeating the same phrase like an echo. When it wasn't a leak from the toilet tank, it was an invasion of ants steaming in along the window frame, the jammed lock on the door, a lamp that wouldn't turn on, or the distorted images on the TV screen whose mystery (Was it the antenna? Was it the TV itself? Was it some kind of interference?) seemed unfathomable. "In a house you never finish, and if you don't take care it'll finish you," was Carmen's contribution to the popular saying.

In the evenings, Carmen and Manolo would rest from their daily chores, seated on the porch, and make a checklist of tasks—those done and those yet to do. They would bring the list of pending items up to date and then elaborate on the strategies to follow.

"Thank God we're retired. That way we can dedicate ourselves completely to the house, because if not it would fall on top of us," joked Manolo, before adding in all seriousness: "It's a lot of house for us Carmen. We should trade homes, find something smaller, *permutar*.*

"I can't believe you said that Manolo. We've been

married for more than forty years and you still don't know me. I'm staying right here because I love this house and because I was born here. My first and only move will be when they take me to the Colón Cemetery."

That was Carmen's response as she sat gazing at the grillwork at the entrance. The rusted inscription, full of arabesques, read, "Villa Nena - 1922." That was the date her grandparents had built their home in the Santos Suárez district.

Ever since Carmen and Manolo's two children married and moved away, the house had been too big for them. That was the reason for Manolo's insistence on looking for a smaller place in better condition. Carmen believed, nevertheless, that no other house would offer the comforts of her own—one that had proved safe from hurricanes and thieves— and was open and well ventilated. And in no other place would she find memories of a lifetime tucked away in all its nooks and crannies.

The drama began to unfold with the torrential downpour on an afternoon in May. At first it seemed like any other rainy afternoon the couple had faced. They closed the windows and doors, and without suspecting what would soon happen, sat down on the porch to enjoy the pleasing smell of wet earth and the cool freshness that the rain brought.

"Tell me the truth, Manolo, do you think there's any other place where we could be enjoying a spectacle like this without worrying about a single drop of rain entering the house?"

"Yes, such a place exists and for sure there's one smaller than this. What we need to do is look for it," he said, sticking to his idea.

"Like ours, don't bet on it," was Carmen's categorical conclusion.

Night fell and the rain intensified instead of letting up. A thick curtain of rain drowned the delicate grass of the flowerbeds.

The increase in the level of water didn't trouble them. They were protected by being five steps above the ground and not even all the water from the hurricane of forty-four, had managed to get that high, Carmen remembered.

They entered the kitchen without suspecting how well they would remember each detail of what happened next. While Manolo was preparing the salad, she began to warm the casserole of rice and heat up some oil in the frying pan to cook eggs. An explosive crackle and a splash of hot oil made Carmen exclaim:

"Manolo, you've done it again! You've left the slotted spoon from lunch in the frying pan and now everything's splattered with oil."

"But you were the one who…" Another explosion interrupted Manolo's protest. "Careful don't burn yourself."

Carmen brandished a pot cover as a shield, put it on top of the frying pan and waited. She felt a different hissing and something wet and didn't understand at first what was happening. She stood watching drops fall on the cover and roll off, making it look like a fountain. Then Manolo's voice, trying to tell her something about the lettuce, and seeming very far away, took her out of her hypnotic state. She traced the trajectory of the drops, searching for their origin. The drama began in earnest with that first shout of horror.

"A leak, Manolo! Look up there, a leak!"

That night they tossed and turned and didn't sleep much. Carmen couldn't stop speculating about the reasons for and consequences of the leak in the kitchen. Manolo tried to calm her by minimizing the importance of what had happened, but his words had little effect.

"It's raining more inside than out," complained Carmen. From the bedroom they could hear, long after it had stopped raining outside, the steady drip, drip, drip of water into the pan on the stove.

When they got up, they faced the situation with optimism and decided to take the bull by the horns. They left the alarm phase behind them and went straight into repair mode—divided into two stages. First, evaluate the damages and then staunch them. Manolo went to their "spare" room, full of chairs that had come unglued and useless items like the hard hats Manolo had used before he retired. He managed to find the ladder and, with Carmen's help in keeping it steady as he went up, he reached the roof.

"Careful, Manolo! Don't get near the eaves or the electric cable! Don't get tangled up in the antenna!" begged Carmen.

"OK, I see what happened," said Manolo cheerfully, as if discovering the cause of the problem would solve it. There're some broken tiles and that's how the water got in. It's easy, Carmita, I can fix it myself with a mixture of cement and sand."

But it wasn't so easy. To get cement and sand cost them, God, only knows how much help and a pile of money, and they could only get what they needed thanks to a black market trafficker. Manolo worked one entire morning filling the open cracks and getting logistical help from Carmen. Two days later when there was a cloudburst, the dripping began again.

Once they got past feeling disappointed about their failure they opted for the asphalt plan. It was suggested by a friend, who gave them an ample amount, explained how to use it, and offered his endorsement based on once having applied it with success. They made a fire in the middle of the patio and heated up the doughy mass until it was a boiling liquid. Then Manolo spread it over the damaged surface, being careful not to burn himself climbing up the ladder quickly with the hot can. Despite their efforts, the asphalt plan also proved a failure, and meanwhile the dripping was turning into a cascade.

Carmen, who used to like rainy days and counted among her most precious memories going out to take rainbaths with her grandmother, grew to hate rain. She became obsessed with listening to the radio for the early morning weather report hoping that the meteorologist would predict good weather. And she cursed if, after a sunny forecast, she saw even a few drops of water on the patio—the same fondly-remembered patio that was part of the refrain of her childhood songs.

They sought out specialized help from old Evelio, a neighbor with bricklaying experience who was proud of having participated in the construction of the "Focsa" building. "It was the tallest structure in Havana in the fifties," bragged Evelio and, "it still is half a century later." Displaying an incredible agility for an octogenarian, Evelio climbed up to the top of the roof, and then rendered his judgment. It was a verdict that left no room for appeal.

"You'll have to take off all the tiles, and I mean all of them. And then you have two ways to solve the problem. Either put on new ones or apply a waterproof coating to the surface. Any other solution will be here today and gone tomorrow, because most of the tiles are calcinated, and at any given moment water can trickle through wherever it wants. One thing's for sure: this type of work costs a lot of money, and aside from that the materials aren't available even in your dreams."

"There's another solution," added Manolo when he and Carmen were alone. "Let's trade houses and leave the leaky roof and the other problems behind."

"Don't bug me about that, Manolo. Can't you see that I've had enough aggravation? Call Holguín and Matanzas, talk to the boys and see how they can help us," she countered.

The boys, now fully grown men, were very concerned and agreed to cover the costs but they couldn't be there for the repairs because both of them had responsibilities at work that could not be postponed.

It was a very rainy month of May. So much so that several precipitation records for the city were broken. In Carmen and Manolo's kitchen new leaks developed along with a menacing spongy-looking spot. The two of them, day by day, broke their own records for the number of pots and pans set up to catch the drips and the number of fruitless measures undertaken to end the nightmare.

One of those days of innumerable comings and goings in search of waterproofing material, they returned home with empty hands only to find the floor of the kitchen flooded because of the overflow from one of the pots.

"Ay Manolo, what's happened to our life?" complained Carmen, remembering the saying 'If it rains, it has to stop raining.' "But it hasn't stopped raining!" she said.

"Don't worry Carmita. I'll get it dry. Go the porch until I call you." And without waiting a moment he picked up the very full cooking pot and headed to the sink trying not to spill any more water on the floor.

She was just leaving the kitchen when she heard him slip.

The time of the fall seemed both brief and interminable to Carmen. It happened so fast that she couldn't help her husband keep his balance. And yet it was so slow that she could imagine herself facing the tragedy of a mortal blow and lamented her stubbornness in remaining in a house where she couldn't imagine living without Manolo.

"Oh honey, speak to me, tell me something," begged Carmen trying to lift him up.

"It's really nothing, Carmita: a little fall and a whack on the ribs," he responded trying to get himself up and running a hand over the part that hurt.

"Manolo, listen, listen to what I'm going to tell you." Carmen took a deep breath and continued: "We're going to move. We can't face all this. The most important thing is staying alive.

But what did they know about *permutas*, switching residences? They'd heard some dreadful stories about people who gathered at the intersection of Prado and Refugio. It was supposed to be a spot where dozens, hundreds of people interested in exchanging houses met up. And of course they had seen it in the movie about house switching, *Se permuta.*

Like flies drawn to honey, those interested in the house knocked on the door, anxious to see the place described as available in the flier hung from the garden railing. Manolo was in charge of showing them the good features of the house, and he had a long discourse prepared for when they ended the tour in the kitchen.

"And here we have a little problem with the roof—easily fixed—but since we've decided to *permutar* we haven't bothered to get it taken care of."

For her part, Carmen stayed away from the showings. That way she wasn't obliged to listen to the *permutantes,* the prospective swappers, enumerate the defects of her house, nor see the feigned indifference on their faces, a strategy practiced so they'd have a certain advantage when it came time to close the deal. Manolo, always good-natured, never lost his aplomb and smiled at everyone, even the aberrant types who came just to see what the house was like on the inside and compare it to their own.

Carmen prepared a booklet where she wrote down the addresses of the houses that, from what they could tell, seemed acceptable. So she wouldn't get discouraged, Manolo went to see the prospective residences as a sort of advance guard and scratched off the list the supposed "doll houses" with nothing to repair and "in a quiet neighborhood," that turned out to be uninhabitable hovels surrounded by noise. Carmen visited the ones that seemed close to their aspirations, but always with a cautious approach.

"We have to take this very slowly, Manolo. We're talking about a house for the rest of our lives."

She ended up rejecting many options. Meanwhile the rains continued wreaking havoc and the fear of dying from a falling chunk of ceiling increased, until one day Carmen saw a place where she knew she could live without regretting too much the loss of her beloved house. It was just what they needed: a spacious living room-dining room, a bedroom with a wall-to-wall closet, the bath and kitchen recently re-tiled, a patio with covered wash tubs, and a little porch where they could continue the tradition of early evening conversations.

The *permutantes*, the exchangers, were a married couple with two children and wanted to get the ball rolling as quickly as possible. They didn't register misgivings about anything, not even the poor condition of the kitchen.

Evidently they had energy and money for repairs and looked at all the possibilities in the house as if they were already owners. They talked about their projects in front of Carmen and Manolo, who listened, feeling perplexed, to all the plans that the family seemingly could carry out with ease. They moved walls, changed colors, closed windows, arranged the furniture and built a stairway to the roof where they planned to put a bedroom/study with a bathroom and a terrace.

"And we couldn't even fix a leak," lamented Carmen.

When the moment came to specify the legal steps, they received the news.

"Well," said the *permutante*, the swapper, to the older couple, "we have a few difficulties to discuss. In the first place, since your house is much bigger than the other, it'll be difficult, the way the law reads, for them to grant an exchange like this one without a special permission that would require months of paperwork." Besides, continued the *permutante*, "We're not the owners of the house that you saw."

"What are you saying?" said Manolo with surprise.

"…We're going to buy it."

"And isn't the purchase and sale of homes prohibited?" asked Carmen.

"It was and it is," intervened the *permutante*. "We live in an apartment on the fifth floor—something not suitable for the two of you. We'll buy the house you saw from a cousin of mine and request permission to exchange, two for one, our apartment and my cousin's house for yours. That way we kill two birds with one stone: we have legal coverage for the purchase of the house and there's no disproportion between the residences because your big house can be exchanged, *permutada*, for two.

"Actually three birds with one stone," added the

permutante, "because my sister would keep the little apartment."

In the face of all the questions, the *permutantes* evidenced a complete knowledge of the topic, citing articles, clauses, and statements of "whereas" and "therefore" of the Housing Law. At last, and like someone who has forgotten something of minor importance, the *permutante* said: "Of course we'll present the application of two for one, alleging a division of joint property, so prior to that you two should get divorced."

"Get divorced?" they both exclaimed.

"Don't worry. It's a divorce only on paper. If you don't, how could you obtain the authorization to *permutar* for two?" pointed out the *permutante.* He added: "You would live together of course, but Carmen would be the owner of the house and Manolo of the apartment. Then my sister marries Manolo, on paper, just on paper. After a little while they divorce, Manolo gives the ownership of the apartment to her and you two can get married again."

Carmen and Manolo felt like they were hallucinating and asked for a couple of days to think it over before giving a definitive answer, even though the others were insistent about going to the notary the very next day.

That afternoon it rained a lot, as much as the afternoon that the leak was first discovered. Feeling discouraged, Carmen and Manolo analyzed a thousand times over the proposition put forward by the *permutantes.*

"It's preposterous, Manolo. Why would we get divorced at this stage of our lives? And worse yet, you'll look like a dirty old man hitched up with a young girl. What would people say?"

"Well, if there's no other solution, I'll have to play my

part," Manolo said jokingly. But another worry was weighing on him. "The problem is... I've been thinking—although I don't really want to talk about it— what would happen if you die before we remarry and I'm not the owner of the house but rather of the little apartment that really isn't mine?"

"Oh honey, I can't stand to think of you out on the street. No, we can't *permutar* under those conditions. I'd rather die in my bed from a falling chunk of ceiling than live with the worry of leaving you forsaken."

"I feel the same way, that is to say, I prefer not to *permutar* under those conditions."

"Well, then, let's close this chapter and get something to eat, because this rain looks like it'll never let up and another deluge awaits us inside."

They reached the threshold of the kitchen and took in the pitiful scene: water falling into receptacles spread out on the stove, the table and the floor.

"You know Carmita, I've just thought of a solution. When we go to the kitchen, we'll put on the hard hats I stored in the spare room after I retired. And if it's raining, we'll use our rainwear."

Carmen looked at him trying to figure out if that was another of Manolo's jokes. But no, he was serious. After a few moments she agreed.

"Good idea. At least that way our heads will be protected and we won't catch a cold. What do you say we take the hat rack from the living room and hang it here so we'll have the head gear and raincoats handy? The bad thing is we'll have to find some really strong nails to support the weight. My mother was sure right. In a house you never finish and if you don't take care…"

"No, Carmita," interrupted Manolo, "this house is not going to finish us, because when it rains, we'll provide the sunshine. We may be stuck with a bad roof but we've got good rainwear and a good way to protect our heads."

With that they set off to look for their "protective" attire and to decide which colors each one should wear. And then Manolo and Carmen were ready to enter the kitchen.

*permutar—This word and its derivatives (*permuta, permutante(s), se permuta* etc.] describes a peculiarly Cuban approach to housing. People don't own private property and can't buy and sell residences. The only way to move is thorough an exchange that is governed by a complicated legal process.

THE TRIP

Inés looked up at the façade of the Colón Cemetery with its
entry arches crowned by a frontispiece representing death,
and felt overwhelmed. For the first time in her life she was
entering the cemetery in Havana. All of her kinfolk were
buried in Guanabacoa, where her family was from and where
they had always lived.

She followed the directions given by her neighbor,
Conchita. "There's no way you'll get lost. You go in through
Zapata and Twelfth Street and follow the avenue as far as the
church. To your left on a parallel street, you'll find the tomb
of *La Milagrosa*, the most visited burial site in the city."
Although Inés had been forewarned, she seemed surprised
by the number of people at the tomb. "Take her flowers. She
likes flowers." Inés' modest cluster of carnations seemed
ridiculous compared to the magnificent array of gladiolas,
deep red roses, and orchids that adorned the headstone and
the surrounding area. "You have to take your place in line
and wait. She can't have too many people making requests at
the same time." Inés discreetly figured out who was last in
line and stood behind a tall, well-dressed man wearing dark
glasses, who appeared to be about forty years old. "Pay
attention to what the others are doing and follow the ritual."
Inés observed that the visitors approached the tomb from

the right side, placed their flowers, stopped to look at the statue of *La Milagrosa*, knocked on the tombstone with one of its brass rings, as if calling to her, and began to pray. "Make your request with lots of faith and never turn your back on her, because if you do you won't be in her favor." When their prayer requests were over, the visitors made a turn about the vault and then stepped away without ceasing to look at the marble effigy.

"Is it true that she performs miracles?" asked Inés of the man in the dark glasses.

"Miracles, I don't know about miracles, but it appears that she grants requests," he responded. "Look at all the inscriptions of thanks accompanying the flowers. They have signatures and dates, and you'll see how many "Thank you, Amelia" messages there are."

"*La Milagrosa* was named Amelia?"

"Yes, Amelia Goyri de Adot. She died en 1901. They say that she died while pregnant yet on the day of the exhumation she was intact with her stillborn child on her breast."

"You don't say," commented Inés to keep the conversation alive. The man told her several anecdotes that gave testimony to the powers of *La Milagrosa*.

"If I'm not being indiscrete, what brought you here?" asked the man.

"I came to ask on behalf of Ramiro. He's my only son," responded Inés. "He's never given me any problems, not even when he was young, and I brought him up practically alone after the divorce. But these days he walks around all stirred up as if he had the devil inside him. He even wants to quit his job as a mechanic. It's all because of the uproar that's been raised over the trip to Canada."

"What trip was that?" he inquired.

"They say that in the Canadian Embassy they're giving visas to those who want to go there for two years to pick apples. A group of boys in the neighborhood is all excited. You know how kids are. They don't care about the cold or anything."

"How interesting. I hadn't heard about…" He left the sentence unfinished because it was now his turn. "Let's talk about it later. I'll wait for you."

When it was time for Inés to approach the tomb, she placed the carnations at the feet of the image of Amelia leaning against a cross, about to give birth. She observed the signs giving thanks for favors: for health, for home, for travel. She concentrated and prayed.

"*Milagrosa*, help Ramiro see the light. If that trip is to his benefit, then let him have it. But if not, keep him from going. It is sacrifice enough that we would be separated and he'd have to work like a mule. On top of that he might be mistreated or have something bad happen there. I'd rather he keep on repairing locomotives even though we don't even have a place to be buried when we die. What I want more than anything in this world, and I ask it of you, is for my son to be happy wherever he is. *Virgencita*, if you grant this to me I promise you the most beautiful flower arrangement you've ever seen, and the card on it will read: 'Thank you Amelia for Ramiro's happiness.' And for a whole year I will bring you flowers every Sunday. I won't miss a single one so that you can be happy, too."

Inés withdrew, without turning her back on *La Milagrosa*, until she bumped into the man with the dark glasses.

"You never know where fortune may find you. You came

here to make a request on behalf of your son, and destiny has put me in your path so that I can help solve your problem," he said. And, noting the curiosity in Inés' eyes, he took off his glasses before continuing. "I'll explain it to you in a minute, but first let me introduce myself, Leobardo Velasco."

"Pleased to meet you Leonardo," she said.

"It's Leobardo not Leonardo. It's Leobardo with a *b*."

"What a strange name. I've never heard it before. My name is Inés, Inés Rodríguez, at your service."

"Delighted to meet you Inés. Listen, I said that I could help you because I have an agreement I'm handling, and we need people willing to work in Maracaibo."

Leobardo continued the explanation as they left the cemetery and walked toward the bus stop. According to him, a friend of his, a member of the Christian Council of Churches in Venezuela, had asked him to handle a contract to bring three hundred young men to work in petroleum exploration as part of a campaign of solidarity with Cuba.

The monthly salary would be about four hundred dollars. Leobardo had obtained the required authorizations; he only needed to complete the selection.

Inés almost felt like she should pinch herself to find out if she were dreaming. It wasn't the same to set out on some venture offered through an embassy, without official support, as it was to take a trip organized through the government.

"We have to be careful and select the people wisely," emphasized Leobardo. "It is vital to create a good impression right from the start, because that will guarantee the continuation of the contract. Here's my telephone. Tell your son to call me any workday before ten o'clock. If he's serious, like you say he is, he could become part of the group."

"Is he serious? Listen, you'd have a hard time finding another one like him. You'll see."

Inés was both agitated and euphoric by the time she got home.

"Son, it's a miracle! You're going to Venezuela. No apples, no cold. Caribbean sunshine and black gold! Thanks to *La Milagrosa*! Well, first thanks to God for guiding Conchita to show me the road to Amelia."

It was hard for Ramiro to get his mother to explain her ideas in a coherent fashion, but when he managed to understand, he got so nervous that he made her repeat the story several times from beginning to end. When they'd calmed down they discussed if they should contact Leobardo the next day or wait a bit before doing it. It was a debate between the fear of losing the opportunity and the disadvantage of showing themselves to be too interested. Heart ruled over reason, although with a certain restraint. Ramiro would not call at eight, like they'd wanted, but would wait until nine thirty the following morning.

The rest of the day they spent making lists of all the things they could get with the astronomical amount of dollars that they could already feel in their pockets and that would vastly increase their income. Number one on the list of appliances was a washing machine "so you won't spend so much work, *mamá*." Next was a rechargeable lamp. No more blackouts in this house! A refrigerator. "I'm tired of the old fridge. It's as old as you are, Ramiro." Two upright fans, "No more mornings looking for a bit of coolness on the porch." And a television set, "because the soap operas look so good in color." They also made lists for home repairs, clothing and shoes, furniture, household goods, and gifts. "Our worries are over." But the list that they thought about with most care was that of the names of friends that Ramiro would suggest if Leobardo gave him the opportunity to include them in the project. "You have to help your neighbor."

"Think carefully about the names you're proposing, Ramiro. You don't want there to be some problem and then you look bad," advised Inés. "And don't even think about saying anything to them until you've spoken with Leobardo."

Neither of them went to work that Monday. They sat in front of the telephone and talked about the trip until Ramiro called. Leobardo himself answered the phone, and without letting much conversation elapse arranged for a meeting that afternoon.

"I'll be waiting for you at five o'clock at the main door of the Ministry of Economic Collaboration, where I work." And after telling him just how to get there, he specified: "I'll be wearing a blue guayabera with short sleeves and jeans, and I carry a briefcase that I never let go of even when I'm sleeping. It'll be easy to recognize me.

Inés helped Ramiro pick out the clothing he'd wear to the appointment.

"Make a good impression. I say that from experience. And be sure to arrive at five on the dot, like well-brought up people—not before and not after. Good luck, son. I'll be here praying to *La Milagrosa* for you."

Inés knew that everything had turned out well when she heard the noise Ramiro made as he closed the door. Now all she needed was to hear the details.

"Tell me, Ramiro. I want to know everything down to the last detail."

Leobardo had asked Ramiro many questions about his

schooling, the places he had worked, and his personal aspirations. Then he had talked to him about the project. He emphasized that conditions would be tough, that it was for real men and that it would not be possible to stay in Venezuela for more than five years because of an agreement between the two governments.

"I told him that I'm not afraid of work and that it's not my intention to leave the country permanently. I'd just like to help solve our economic difficulties."

"Did you talk to him about the other boys?" asked Inés.

"Well sure. And know what? Leobardo asked me if I would be something like his secretary in that matter. He says that if *La Milagrosa* facilitated the meeting between the two of you then he trusts me. He has close to one hundred already enrolled and he wants me to help him find the rest of the group. When I have the people located, he'll get together with us and make the selection."

"And when will the trip be?"

"It'll have to be soon because they're waiting for us there. Two or three months at the most.

"What luck we've had Ramiro, what luck!"

The first person to find out about the plans was Conchita, who jumped for joy, seeing a chance opening up for her own son, Agustín. On the other hand, Pedro, her husband was not enthusiastic.

"I can't believe, Conchita, that you're being so gullible. It's very unlikely that they'd choose our boys. No doubt the guy said that to Inés because they were in the cemetery with *La Milagrosa* in front of them. Just wait and see how this dream turns to ashes."

Inés and Ramiro asked for vacation time and turned the house into a recruiting station. Helped by Conchita and

Agustín, they worked out a scheme of "requirements" for the candidates. They should be: single men, from twenty-five to thirty years old, healthy, with a minimum educational level of twelfth grade or else graduates in technology and with work experience of five years or more. They contacted family members and good friends who, then, offered the names of close friends and relatives, who in turn contacted others who contacted others. All were asked to maintain absolute discretion and to inform only those who met the stipulated conditions. Three days of intense bustling about yielded a balance of a hundred and eighty-six aspirants. That night while they were taking stock of the situation, Agustín threw in the bombshell:

"Mother and I are worried about something. We've been thinking that if we present Leobardo with more than two hundred people, like he asked, so that he could choose, when the time comes to make the cut, some of us, that is to say from our group, might be left out."

"There're a lot of engineers and college grads on the list, and for all we know he might prefer the ones with those qualifications," noted Conchita. "So we'll have to act very carefully."

"Those who'll be left out are going to be left out, don't you doubt it," said Pedro, with his habitual pessimism.

Neither Inés nor Ramiro had thought about that, convinced as they were that Ramiro would be chosen. After a few seconds of consternation, Inés said:

"Well look, let's turn around the conventional wisdom and that'll be it: in our case it's better too have too few than too many. We'll present the ones we have thus far and not one more, and he can find the others himself." And thus the list was finished.

Ramiro breathed a sigh of relief when Leobardo congratulated him. They decided to have the meeting with the candidates the following Sunday. Although it would be more tiring to do it that way, they agreed to divide up the group into three parts to avoid confusion and facilitate communication. They set the times at nine, ten and eleven in the morning. Ramiro would find an adequate locale close to his house and would make the appointments staggered. Leobardo would be there, without fail, at eight thirty, to have coffee with Inés.

"The house best suited for the meetings is Conchita's because it has a large terrace with a roof," suggested Inés to Ramiro. "Besides, who better than she to welcome Leobardo?"

Conchita accepted with delight and promised to scout up chairs in the neighborhood. "The boys are not going to be left standing up." She also promised a good table that would serve as desk for Leobardo, "set with an elegant white embroidered tablecloth."

From early in the morning, Inés, Conchita and their sons were prepared to receive Leobardo. Pedro, always a skeptic, preferred to act as rearguard and stayed inside the house. Every once in a while Ramiro would go out to the street.

"I hope he doesn't leave us stranded," said Agustín at close to eight thirty.

"Don't worry about it. He'll be here," assured Inés.

"And if he gets lost?" worried Conchita.

"How can he get lost? I gave him the address, and besides he has the telephone number here," responded Ramiro.

Displaying a perfect English punctuality, Leobardo arrived just at the agreed upon hour. After the introductions and coffee, Leobardo wanted to know if they had acted with the necessary caution, which would help avoid setbacks.

"Everything's been thought through," replied Inés. "Each group will wait for its turn in the nearby houses, and when we give the signal they'll come to Conchita's. We've made it clear that only the ones already on the list can come—no companions, no last minute additions. Pedro, Agustín's father, will be at the entrance to guarantee order."

There was remarkable discipline in the three meetings guided with assurance and precision by Leobardo: the presentation of the labor contract terms, which took about fifteen minutes, a half an hour to clear up any doubts, and last of all an explanation of the procedure to be followed.

"Now, you'll need to fill out a form that I'll be handing out. Within approximately a week, you'll know if you've been chosen by the Ministry of Economic Collaboration. The ones selected should submit, through Ramiro, one hundred pesos and six passport-type photos for the immigration transactions. Once the documents are issued, the candidates should go individually to the Venezuelan Embassy to get the visa, whose cost—forty five dollars—will be covered by the Ministry. Most likely the trip would be via a charter flight, originating in Venezuela.

Leobardo did not accept Inés' invitation to lunch but did accede to the request to sit at the head of the table, which was modest but well served. There, Leobardo was accompanied by the morning welcoming party, along with Pedro. Following the after-lunch conversation, in which they talked about the powers of *La Milagrosa*, Leobardo took his leave, expressing appreciation for their help and noting:

"We must continue to maintain the same discretion

observed until now. I'll come by again after I've had a chance to study the list."

Before the week was out, Leobardo had concluded his analysis and discussed the results with Inés and Ramiro.

"You have really smoothed the way for me with the pre-selection process, so that practically the entire group qualifies. I'm only doubtful about these five," he said, showing them the dubious applications. "It's hard to believe that with so many spelling errors they have the degree of education that they claim. It really doesn't matter to me if they write well or not since we're not hiring them as scribes. What's unacceptable is deceit."

"If you trust me with this, I'll check everything out so we won't have any lingering doubts," suggested Ramiro

"Perfect. Then what's left is to collect the money and the photos, and you'll take care of that, Ramiro. Ask them to put the photos in an envelope with the name written clearly outside. If you want you can give them a receipt. And when everything's turned in you can call me—like always—before ten and I can come by in one of the office cars. It's dangerous to carry that much money on a bus.

Seventy-two hours later, Inés and Ramiro turned over to Leobardo the eighteen thousand six hundred pesos and the photos. Ramiro noted:

"The five questionable ones are included. I interviewed them, and I'll guarantee them even though they have spelling errors even when they speak."

"As I said earlier, I have full confidence in you, Ramiro. Now I've got to run because the driver is waiting. Tomorrow I'll present the dossiers to Immigration before leaving for Guantánamo, a trip I've been postponing. I'll be there fifteen to twenty days, and as soon as I get back, I'll pick up the passports and I'll call you."

"Thank you Leobardo. You're our guardian angel. I don't know how to thank you. May *La Milagrosa* guide and protect you always, just as you deserve." Inés said goodbye to Leobardo almost in tears and with a big hug.

A month went by and there was no word from Leobardo. Ramiro and Inés began to feel a growing pressure on them when dozens of those selected came by their house daily asking if they knew anything about the trip. They called Leobardo several times by telephone and nobody answered.

"It must be broken because it's in a workplace, and it's odd that nobody answers," said Inés, trying to figure it out.

"And why hasn't he come by? asked Agustín with misgiving in his voice.

"Maybe he's sick or there's some complication in Guantánamo," said Conchita.

"I thought it seemed fishy from the beginning," said Pedro, and the conversation repeated itself until Ramiro declared:

"I'm going to ask for him at the Economic Collaboration offices."

But nobody there knew a Leobardo Velasco, either by name or by the description that Ramiro, in desperation, gave to the receptionist.

"A swindler?! No, Ramiro, it has to be a mistake," insisted Inés, refusing to accept the evidence.

"I told you so, I told you so," repeated Pedro.

"What a first class S.O.B.!" exclaimed Conchita. "But, he'll have to pay for it. He played not only us but also *La Milagrosa*, and that's going to really cost him."

It was Conchita who convinced Inés to go to the Colón

Cemetery. "We're going to put this ne'er-do well in the hands of *La Milagrosa,* and she'll take care of him." And so they went together to the most visited tomb in Havana.

When they got there, they immediately noticed a huge bouquet, showy, full of flowers and still fresh. The inscription, which they read, perplexed, was a message with Leobardo's signature. It said: "Thank you Amelia for the trip."

I'LL EXPLAIN IT TO YOU

To Miguel García
  He knows why

By early evening it appeared that we'd known each other forever. It hardly seemed possible that we had conversed for the first time in our lives on a hot Monday morning under the shade of the mango trees in my patio.

Saying "the first time in our lives" is an exaggeration, because Raúl and I are cousins. Until the time that we separated at the end of first grade, we lived fairly close by and were playmates, at least so they said. Now after almost four decades of not seeing each other, we mostly remembered what we'd been told rather than what we could actually recall.

"You used to get really cross, cousin, when they made you sing," said Raúl.

"And you're the one who didn't want to go in the water at the beach and just made sand castles. Remember?"

Ever since Raúl went to Miami, we kept up with each other through our mothers, who wrote back and forth and talked on the telephone frequently. Then about five years ago the lines of communication broke down, after the death of my aunt Esther and mother's passing away a few months later.

The call from Raúl the day before we got together had made me a little nervous. He was in a hotel in Havana and said that he wanted to see me. But what would we talk about?

Now with Raúl in front of me, after the first moments of kisses and hugs and a mutual nervousness, it occurred to me to break the ice with a photo session. I dusted off the old family album, handed down from grandmother, and Raúl looked through it very attentively as he listened to the comments I made about each photograph. He had never seen himself in diapers or at a kid's carnival dressed up as a peasant boy with a machete at his belt and a mustache and sideburns. And he'd never seen what his mother looked like when she was a child.

His family's departure—by the seat of their pants—from Camarioca was so rushed that aunt Esther told Raúl that they didn't have time to gather up the chunks of memory that are preserved by photos and letters. I omitted mentioning to Raúl that his grandparents' remorse meant that they never put those last images of him, in Cuba, in the album. They preferred to keep the pictures of the departure day—which showed Raulito headed north and wearing a coat and long pants— in an envelope tucked away in the closet.

We chased away the sadness of the nostalgic albums by making fun of how we looked in the silly poses that adults made us assume for our birthday parties and by laughing at the stagy formality in the photos of our ancestors. I also showed him the photos of my daughter's fifteenth birthday party, pointing out how much she resembled Aunt Esther as a young woman. For his part, he pulled out of his wallet some glossy, color photographs of his wife and children that he always carried with him.

We talked about the relatives here and there, of the

dreams that had been fulfilled and the ones yet to be realized and about our likes and dislikes. As the time went by, I was surprised at how well Raúl and I understood each other. Nobody would have said that he hadn't lived in Havana since way back when, except for his accent, the crutch of saying "you know" all the time and the Miami custom of substituting kinship terms like cousin, auntie, and grandmother for proper names. We Cubans are the same on both shores, say what they will, I thought.

Everything was going like clockwork until Raúl stood up and asked:

"Cousin, can I use your bathroom?"

It is only now that I understand that my mistake was in saying too much. I should only have told him that if he used the toilet he should turn on the little bypass valve located below the water tank of the toilet itself so that it would flush. That's all I should have said and nothing more. In fact, I started with just that but the puzzled look on Raúl's face made me add:

"It has a leak because the supply valve doesn't close. We've thought of substituting a piece of Styrofoam for the rubber float."

It was obvious he didn't understand, so for the sake of friendship I decided to offer him more details.

"Look, I'll explain it to you, Raulito. The original float got cracked, water gets in and so it doesn't float; and therefore the supply valve doesn't work as a stopper. A cube of Styrofoam, compact and light, would last forever—the perfect solution.

"A cube…" said Raúl, and I saw the effort he was making to untangle my words.

"I said a cube because it's easy to make with Styrofoam.

The importance is not the form but using a material that floats and can go down with the water. Then at a certain point the valve closes. If not the tanks keep emptying and we end up all dried up until they give us water again"

"What do you mean until they *give* you water again?" he asked, waiting for my reply. I realized that he was trying hard to understand.

"Well, since water is scarce, what happens is they give it to us at certain intervals, depending on the level of El Gato reservoir, which is the one that provides water for this neighborhood. In this dry period, we get eight hours of water every three days. I'll give you an example: tomorrow, Tuesday, we get water from two in the afternoon until ten at night, and then we won't get more water until Friday. That's why we store it," I said pointing toward the tanks located on the roof and next to the washtub.

If at that moment Raúl had gone to the bathroom, the discussion would have ended. But he remained seated looking at the pipes that ran up and down, the spigots along the way, the hoses, and the buckets. I supposed that he admired the engineering work and, I confess, I let myself get carried away by vanity.

"It was my husband Alfredo's idea. He loves plumbing. Here, let me explain how it works."

I took him over to the washtub and there under the noonday sun I began to expound on the philosophy of the system:

"We collect water in those three fifty-five gallon drums that function like a cistern. Because let me tell you that to make a hole big enough for a real cistern in this rocky terrain would mean a lot of problems. But that's beside the point," I said, while Raúl checked out the storage tanks mounted on blocks on the floor to the side of the washtub. He bent over to test the stability of the large mass of metal. "As you can see, the pipes reach this tank and then, through the principle of connecting containers, the water runs through these hoses to the other tanks. With a turbine we pump the water to the two tanks on the roof. As long as the water arrives as scheduled and the tanks below are full, there's no problem." This last statement let slip the fact that the system had a weak point.

"The water doesn't always get this far…," said Raúl placing his hand on one of the tanks. He seemed disillusioned, and by now his shirt was damp with sweat.

"That's right," I had to acknowledge.

"And then, cousin?" Raúl had a look of sincere worry on his face and seemed a little weary—which I attributed to the heat.

"We solve that with a "water burglar," I said with conviction.

"A water burglar?" he asked sounding alarmed.

"I'll explain it to you, Raulito," I said, wanting to make sure that he understood. It's the name we give to a type of turbine that not only pumps water up but sucks it in. If you connect it to where the plumbing enters the house, it pulls the water from the neighborhood to us. The problem is if we were to get it and install it—which wouldn't be easy— we would be taking water from our neighbors, and we don't really want to do that."

"So then, cousin?" Raulito seemed really worn out. I remembered what grandmother said every time she talked about the day that Raulito and his parents left. "That poor little boy was in a cold sweat, no doubt from fright."

"You see the little spigot right here? Fortunately it always gets water, that is, when there is water. And all Alfredo and I have to do is carry it in buckets to fill the tanks." I said this last part fast and added: "We pump it upstairs and that's it, unless there's a blackout."

I saw that Raúl was completely overwhelmed, and I tried to lift his spirits.

"All in all, it's not such a big problem, Raulito. There are people much worse off than we are. It breaks your heart to see those images on television of people walking kilometers to get a little bit of water. One of every five inhabitants on the planet lacks safe drinking water. That's incredible, isn't it? "

Raúl was very quiet, and I was afraid that he might be on the verge of fainting, but just when I was about to ask him what was wrong, he said:

"Cousin, with your permission, I'd like to go to the bathroom. And don't worry. The only thing I want to do is splash a little water on my face."

We went into the house, and he hesitated at the door to the bathroom. I saw in his expression the look of someone who wants to say something but is afraid of giving offense. At last he mustered the courage to inquire:

"Is there any problem with the faucet of the sink?"

That was the only time I contained myself.

"No, Raulito, it works perfectly." I had to bite my tongue because I thought: How in the world could I explain it to him? After years of having a leaky faucet we'd found a solution. It turns out that the best washer for a leaky faucet is the little rubber ring that you can find fitted inside the top of a bottle of penicillin.

CLOSED FOR REPAIRS

He had won the distinction of being considered a highly competent man in the *Poder Popular* (People's Voice) provincial office of the city of Havana. He was known as a worker, a man with a talent for finding solutions to the most unusual problems. And now, Ramón had been chosen from among a group of candidates to be the new head of the Department of Community Concerns.

He had barely begun this ombudsman position when he set out to eradicate what he considered some of the "inherited ills" of the previous administration.

With a concerted effort carried out through financial calculations and reports, he obtained authorization for an increase in the number of workers under his control and an official vehicle for his use. The accumulated problems were so many and were of such long standing, Ramón had argued, that they simply couldn't be handled by just three people receiving and routing complaints and suggestions from the community. When he had in place a receptionist, someone to answer the telephone, two people taking down statements, another two to type them up, one more to do the filing, an assistant department head, a secretary, and a car with chauffeur, Ramón knew that he was fully equipped to offer the level of service that the public deserved. The concept of multitasking was applied by asking the receptionist to assume occasional janitorial duties.

Lack of punctuality made Ramón positively sick, even though he knew it was a difficult vice to conquer and one with which he'd been forced to coexist. The least to which we can aspire, he said, is to never give our clientele the vexation of not being waited on promptly. To achieve this aim, he directed that people would be seen between ten in the morning and three in the afternoon, with a break between twelve and one for lunch. Since the work day continued being eight to five, the late arrivals or early departures of his employees would not affect the quintessential function of the department: to serve the public.

One of Ramón's goals was to refurbish the workplace, but his resources were scarce, that is to say, virtually nil. Since architects had assured him that the danger of ceiling collapse in the reception area was minimal as long as the beams that were helping hold it up did not give way, he turned his attention elsewhere. With the help of the subalterns, as he called his underlings, he embellished the offices through a cleanup campaign, decorative touches and ornamental plants, with trailing vines that helped hide the ceiling supports. It's important, he insisted, that people who come here in a state of tribulation, to seek our help feel, when they cross the threshold, like they are in a welcoming place.

Ramón came to know perfectly the most common gripes and how to channel them. We are simply mediators between the people and the executive bureaus, he emphasized, but the steps we take determine to a certain degree if the problems have a chance of getting solved. He personally waited on the recidivists (those who came back to the office when their cases were not resolved), tried to encourage them, and forwarded their requests again.

That's how he came to know Venancio, a grandfather who arrived at Ramón's offices pushing a baby cart with his triplet grandchildren. This happened every time that the deadline for the re-opening of the neighborhood day care center passed and it was still closed for repairs. These children are going to go to that day care center or my name isn't Ramón, the chief promised.

After a year on the job, twleve months into his term of office, Ramón prepared for an inspection by his immediate superior. He did so with confidence, knowing how much they had worked and aware of the encouraging results that had rewarded those efforts. Statistics showed a lessening of the average time it took to handle complaints from fifteen to eight days and an improvement in the index of errors of said transactions from forty to thirty percent. The increase in the number of return cases he interpreted as an expression of confidence on the part of the public who came to the department more than one time seeking help to alleviate their problems.

The day of the announced inspection, Ramón arrived at the department early as usual and closeted himself in his office, after dispatching the chauffeur to get a light snack that he could offer the inspectors. He asked Cusa, the receptionist, who at that time was engaged in the auxiliary clean-up work, not to let anyone bother him. Although the meeting was set for two in the afternoon, and he had had everything ready since the day before, he considered it prudent to look over the documentation he had prepared one more time. He wanted to be able to argue successfully the more complicated cases such as the child care center, which was still closed for repairs.

He was so wrapped up in the paperwork, tables, and graphs showing the achievements that he had obtained that he lost track of time. He looked at the clock, then realized that his secretary wasn't there and was alarmed to see that it was eleven and she hadn't yet arrived. That's odd, he thought. Sometimes she doesn't show up, but she knows how much I need her today.

He called Cusa and found out from her the extent of the disaster. The only ones in the office were the two of them and one of the typists.

"And why didn't you tell me about so many people being absent?" he chided her.

"Because you yourself said not to let anyone bother you," Cusa argued back, and without giving time for his reply she explained the justifications for the various absences. These ranged from the eternal lack of buses and lack of water, to a medical test, a bicycle accident caused by a pothole, the steps being taken for a trip abroad, preparations for a baptism, the need to waterproof the roof of a house, and the sudden illness of a pig being fattened. "Tell me what I'm supposed to do with the people who are waiting outside."

"Well, what else can you do? Simply inform them that today we can't deal with their problems," responded Ramón categorically.

The first thing that occurred to Ramón was to call his boss and cancel the visit, on the pretext that he was suffering chest pains. That turned out to be impossible because the phone was on the blink and could only take incoming calls. He couldn't use the car because the chauffeur hadn't yet

Nancy Alonso

returned, and if he went on foot it destroyed his alibi of the chest pains.

He was still thinking about a solution that would allow him to postpone the visit and get out of the predicament, when Cusa interrupted him.

"All the clientele have gone except for Venancio, the old gentleman of the daycare center closed for repairs. He says he needs to see you for just a moment, and there's no way to get him to leave. Today he came without the triplets."

Ramón was all too familiar with Venancio's insistence and conceded with a tone of resignation:

"OK, let him in."

The old man entered Ramon's office with a cheerful *buenos días* and a broad smile on his face. He placed a package wrapped up in newspapers on the desk.

"I'm bringing you this as a gift," he said, still smiling. "Open it up."

Ramón did so, and there before his eyes was a cracked, moist sign with discolored lettering, done by hand, which read: CLOSED FOR REPAIRS. To his surprise Ramón heard Venancio explain:

"They've re-opened the daycare center. This morning they held the re-inauguration ceremony, and I decided to bring this sign to leave with you as a gesture of my eternal gratitude for all you've done to help us win the battle."

"Well, didn't I tell you that we'd solve the problem, Venancio? You don't need to thank me; I only did what I was charged to do. Now if you'll excuse me I have a lot to," said Ramón, giving the old man a hug.

By himself again, Ramón gave a sigh of relief that he could now cross off the daycare center on his list of problems to solve. He was just playing with the sign in his hands when the idea came to him.

He went to Cusa and the one typist who'd showed up and told them they had the day off. Since no one else was there, there was no way to work, and the inspection wasn't going to be possible. Once the two women, surprised but happy, had left, Ramón put his plan into action.

He took the chain used to hang the fern planter in his office and tied it around one of the support beams in the reception area. Pulling with all his might and with one foot braced on the beam, he managed to displace the wedge underneath the column until the wood began to lean.

Ramón left the building, locked the door, and said to himself "Now let's see what happens," as he put up the sign that said, CLOSED FOR REPAIRS.

NANCY ALONSO, one of Cuba's most acclaimed writers, was born in Havana, in 1949. She currently teaches physiology. Her first book of stories, *Tirar la primera piedra*, was a finalist in the David Competition in 1995. *Closed for Repairs* won the prize for feminist fiction, "Alba de Céspedes," in 2002.

ANNE FOUNTAIN was born in Buenos Aires and earned graduate degrees at Indiana University and Columbia University. She is currently a professor of Latin American literature and culture and coordinator of Latin American Studies at San José State University. Her recent publications include *José Martí and U.S. Writers* (2003) and *Versos Sencillos: A Dual Language Edition* (2005).

Curbstone Press, Inc.

is a non-profit publishing house dedicated to multicultural literature that reflects a commitment to social awareness and change, with an emphasis on contemporary writing from Latino, Latin American, and Vietnamese cultures.

Curbstone's mission focuses on publishing creative writers whose work promotes human rights and intercultural understanding, and on bringing these writers and the issues they illuminate into the community. Curbstone builds bridges between its writers and the public—from inner-city to rural areas, colleges to cultural centers, children to adults, with a particular interest in underfunded public schools. This involves enriching school curricula, reaching out to underserved audiences by donating books and conducting readings and educational programs, and promoting discussion in the media. It is only through these combined efforts that literature can truly make a difference.

Curbstone Press, like all non-profit presses, relies heavily on the support of individuals, foundations, and government agencies to bring you, the reader, works of literary merit and social significance that would likely not find a place in profit-driven publishing channels, and to bring these authors and their books into communities across the country.

If you wish to become a supporter of a specific book—one that is already published or one that is about to be published—your contribution will support not only the book's publication but also its continuation through reprints.

We invite you to support Curbstone's efforts to present the diverse voices and views that make our culture richer. Tax-deductible donations can be made to:
Curbstone Press, 321 Jackson Street, Willimantic, CT 06226
phone: (860) 423-5110   fax: (860) 423-9242
www.curbstone.org